Shana's Marriage

A novel
by Ante Jakšić

translated by
Dubravka Williams-Podhraški
from the original Croatian edition

First published in Great Britain in 2024, on behalf of Mrs Dubravka Williams-Podhraški, by Mil Williams

Copyright for the translation into English from the original Croatian edition © Mrs Dubravka Williams-Podhraški

The right of Mrs Dubravka Williams-Podhraški to be identified as the Translator of this English version of the Work has been asserted by her in accordance with the Copyright, Designs and Patents Act 1988.

All rights reserved. No part of this publication may be reproduced, stored in a retrieval system, or transmitted, in any form or by any means without the prior written permission of the translator herself and/or Mil Williams, nor be otherwise circulated in any form or binding or cover other than that in which it is published and without a similar condition being imposed on the subsequent purchaser.

Paperback ISBN 979 8 340 64827 3

Proofreading and editing services delivered by
https://qcdocu.com/books

Permission to publish the English translation of the original Croatian edition

Permission to publish the English translation of the book „Šana se udaje", published by **Kršćanska sadašnjost** in Zagreb, Croatia, 1980:

Author: Ante Jakšić
Title of the original book: „Šana se udaje"
Publisher and copyright of the 1980 edition used for this translation: Kršćanska sadašnjost d.o.o., Zagreb, Croatia

Dubravka Williams-Podhraški gratefully acknowledges the permission, given by **Kršćanska sadašnjost d.o.o.**, to translate and publish „Šana se udaje" for the English-speaking market, and thanks the publisher for having published the original edition from which the English has been translated.

Image credits
Chapter 1: Colin (Joseph) Williams
Chapter 4: Colin (Joseph) Williams
Chapter 10: Unknown artist (from a woodcut believed to have been bought in Zagreb central market, Croatia)
Chapter 15: Mrs Dubravka Williams-Podhraški

All other images have been used by Mrs Dubravka Williams-Podhraški on the understanding that they have been inherited for free use from her own family and history.

If anyone feels they need to be attributed for the images thus used, please get in touch with Dubravka via the Amazon.co.uk page for "Shana's Marriage".

Every effort has thus been made to establish the copyright of the images used, as described above. Please do get in touch if you have any additional information, so it may be added to future editions.

Contents

Foreword 7
Chapter 1 11
Chapter 2 15
Chapter 3 19
Chapter 4 27
Chapter 5 35
Chapter 6 45
Chapter 7 59
Chapter 8 73
Chapter 9 85
Chapter 10 99
Chapter 11 117
Chapter 12 139
Chapter 13 153
Chapter 14 169
Chapter 15 185
Chapter 16 199
Chapter 17 209
Biography of the Author 217

Foreword

My name is Dubravka A. Williams-Podhraški, née Podhraški. I am the translator of this English version of the lyrical novel, "Shana's Marriage", by Ante Jakšić.

I was born in Druškovec in 1938. Druškovec, Hum na Sutli, is a small village in the northwest of Croatia, and it is relevant to why I found I just had to translate the novel in the first place.

But first some background.

I started my life in the rural community of my mother's father Mr S. Govedić. My family then moved to Varaždin, a city where the family of six, which we were, spent all of World War II. After the war my parents lost their teaching jobs. We were moved to Krapina, where I continued my education at the local Primary School. I then went to High School, and finally on to Zagreb University in 1957 to study English and History of Art.

I visited the UK for the first time in 1959 to perfect my English, returning back to Croatia after a year to continue my studies at Zagreb University for another year.

I married Colin (Joseph) in 1961 in Poredje, Croatia. He was a student of Emmanuel College, Cambridge, and had first visited Krapina in 1957 with his friend Hoppy.

I spent the rest of my life living in the UK near Oxford, where our three sons were born; then from 1967 in Chester, where our twin daughters were born, and to this day. Summer holidays, as Colin (Joseph) was a teacher, were spent almost every year in my Croatian homeland.

I first came across "Shana's Marriage" in 1980 because my uncle Rev. M. J. Govedić, a parish priest, who had a smallholding in Oroslavje for forty years – a similarly rural community to the one portrayed in the book before you – gave me this novel in an original Croatian edition. It was called *"Šana se udaje"*.

The book immediately resonated with me on so many levels. Shana's oppression by the ruling rural society of the time – by those with wealth and power – whilst profoundly different in respect of my own family, mirrored other perceptions I had of my upbringing under the Communist regime of Tito. Freedoms only existed nominally for the outside world and the West, which chose, generally, to turn a blind eye. But for people living in what was then called Yugoslavia, and who were not considered to have approved of the regime, it was quite a different matter.

The literature books generally assert that Jakšić was sidelined and ignored by Communist Yugoslavia because of his deep Catholic faith, but whilst indeed it played a major part, a closer reading of "Shana's Marriage" surely leads us to the firm conclusion that what the regime most feared was the powerful body of Jakšić's ideas – which followed from the Catholic teachings about the just redistribution of wealth and the rights of workers – and well communicated and shaped in this novel in particular, in respect of the rights of every human being to live his life without fear or favour, to the full.

On my first reading of "Shana's Marriage", I loved it so much that I promised my uncle that one day I would like to translate it for all those Croats who have been scattered round the world for so many reasons, and may even have lost the use of their mother tongue.

But equally, for a wider audience too, where freedom continues to be yearned for and truth remains our common touchstone.

I hope therefore that my translation of the book you have in your hands does justice to the power and integrity of Jakšić's thought, prose, and poetry, as well as to your own aspirations for a better life.

Thank you.

Mrs Dubravka Williams-Podhraški

Chester UK, September 2024

Chapter 1

A heavy, silvery morning mist rose over the meadows, the ploughed lands, over the groves and the vast open fields. It rolled like white wheels, evading, bending, encircling and wallowing on the ground, then slowly rising up, all the while becoming thinner and more transparent, like the gossamer silk drapes that blew around the windows on fresh, scented mornings, when the sun rose behind the great cross that had stood for years in the village cemetery on top of the small hill.

Whilst the warm rays of the sun scattered on the dewy grass, on bushes, lairs and open fields, the thin veil of morning mist rose higher and higher, blending with the clear blue sky, which suddenly brightened up over the whole of the lowlands. Whilst the wood that pensively watches over at the end of the village awoke, the sound of a cowman's horn could be heard from the village. This sound seemed to cause unrest amongst the low rural houses huddling together, as the doors began to open quickly, and hogs and large sows streamed out of the yards. A housewife chased them with a short stick that always stood handy near the pigsty. The place was waking up: carts moving in the street and windows opening. In front of the houses everything had already been swept clean, because this task was usually done early, in semi-darkness, whilst the rest of the household still slept.

And when the last cloud of mist had risen and dispersed in the warmth of the rays of the sun, the white-fleeced sheep and lambs appeared bleating behind the bushes, scattering over the damp grass and beginning to graze upon the fresh grass. They were followed by a tall, swarthy and strong young man holding a large shepherd's crook. As soon as the sheep started to graze, the young man leant against a weeping willow whose branches hung low, casting a cool early morning shadow. He stared into the distance and then, as if his heart were troubled, he bowed his head and sighed. His alert sheep-dog sat at his feet and kept watch on his every move, ready to respond immediately to his commands, but at that moment the young man was unaware of his dog and it seemed that his thoughts were not here at all, but elsewhere.

Then a step was heard, the sheep raised their heads, some even ran forwards, but soon they quickly bowed their heads again and carried on grazing.

"Hey, shepherd, how are you?"

A voice filled the fresh morning air. The young man raised his head, his eyes lit up and, gathering his cloak, he called out.

"Marko!"

"Indeed, Marin, it is me. I am on my way to the plum orchard and I noticed you standing there deep in thought. I could not pass by without saying a few words to you."

"It has been a long time since our last meeting."

"And that is why I came. I kept thinking that I would see you, that you would come to the evening circle-dance, but not a peep out of you, as if the earth had swallowed you up. Why don't you come so we can have fun together?"

"What is the point of going there?" Marin shrugged his shoulders.

"And what did you do in the past?"

"In the past?" Marin laughed, and a shadow of sorrow passed over his eyes and flowed down over his ruddy lips.

"You have to come, because Mika Balazhevich is pestering Shana."

"I know."

"And?"

"What can I do, when she is not for me? You have heard what her father says about me."

"I have heard, but you know that she loves you and does not want to hear about Mika at all."

"I know, but for this reason her father does not want to hear about me and he likes Mika."

Marko laughed at these words and came very close to Marin.

"Yesterday I was at the circle-dance with Shana and she had a message for you: she would come down to the garden at midday, so keep a look out for her."

Marin raised his head:

"What about her parents?"

"They will not be at home."

"Okay, tell her that I will wait for her. I will wait for her."

Marko went down the meadow and when he was a fair way off, he turned round, waved his hand and shouted:

"I will make sure that everything goes all right."

Marin carried on watching after him, as if he could not believe that Shana had sent him this message. Suddenly his heart leapt, he closed his eyes wistfully and his hands gripped the cloak more tightly.

"Shana, Shana," he whispered. "It is so hard to be without you. Am I not just as good as anybody, why must I not love you? Why do I have a heart and eyes that make me able to see you?"

The sheep had already moved away and the dog jumped and barked. Marin roused himself from his reverie. He tightened his grip on his shepherd's crook, threw his cloak over his left arm and, having eyed his flock, he slowly followed it.

Chapter 2

"No, you do not love me," said Shana and her eyes clouded. "If you loved me, you would not be as you are now."

Marin leant on the fence, broke off a twig and turned it round in his fingers, playing with it.

"Yes, I know that you have been doubting me recently, but what can I do about that? Who wants to know whether I love you or not? I can love you as much as I like and who cares if I am honest with you? They could not care less about my love!"

He moved away from the fence and averted his face:

"Well, if I had twenty or more acres of land, I would immediately rise in your father's eyes, then he would not mind that 'the pauper's son' loves his daughter! But as it is ..."

Uneasily, Shana came closer to the fence. "But when you said you would never leave me and when I believed you, I was a real fool. How could I have even believed you? Now you do not ask how I feel, how I spend my days, how I weep every night! Now it is all the same to you. To think that I believed you, but now I can see what you are! This is your love. I would have gone to the ends of the earth with you, but you have simply forgotten me!"

She covered her face with her hands, turned round and was about to leave.

"Shana!"

She did not turn around.

His heart ached. He was sad. He was afraid that she would go and would not come back. He was afraid because she had begun to doubt him and this was the hardest thing for him to bear. He quickly jumped over the fence, caught up with her, grasped her shoulders from behind and turned her towards him.

"Shana!"

She looked at the ground.

"Let me go."

"Why are you torturing me? You know that I love you. You can see that I behave in this way because I am afraid it would harm you if I behaved differently. It is because of you that I have stopped coming to the circle-dancing – I could not bear not being with you. Do you understand me? And you reproach me. You reproach me and you do not know how my heart aches for you, how I spend days thinking about you."

He took her hands and stroked her hair.

"Do not be angry with me. Be kind!"

She squeezed his hand firmly and laid her head on his chest.

The garden was redolent with a scent that floated tenderly on the wings of the caressing wind from the dyke across the meadow, a scent that had now stopped to rest in the shade of the garden. The bell of the lead ram and the bleating of the sheep could be heard from the meadow.

"You can see," he said, "how I am battling with myself. I am trying to convince myself that it would be best for me to go somewhere far away, just to avoid being here amongst these people. And if it had not been for you, I would have gone long ago and I would never have come back. Never. And whenever I decide to go, I cannot do it, because I remember you. And now you say that I do not love you, that I am forgetting you! Can you not feel that despite my full faculties, I am going mad?"

"I believe you are good!"

"Shana!"

She raised her head, and then he said:

"If you are not going to be mine, no other will take your place, I swear." He caressed her hair, touched her cheek with his cheek, and at once their lips met, their eyes closed and a warm wave of inexpressible happiness carried them for a moment on its golden wings.

Then, derisive laughter, like a hard blow, startled them out of their embrace.

"Well, well, congratulations!"

They turned round quickly. Mika Balazhevich stood before them holding in his hand a thin, long birch with which he was touching his shiny polished boots.

"You could have carried on," said Mika with bitterness, looking at Marin sullenly.

"This is none of your business," said Marin, turning to leave.

"I am telling you not to come here again," replied Mika.

"Oh, and I should ask your permission!"

"The girl is not for you and therefore you must leave her alone, because otherwise you might find your head pulped!"

"Nobody is going to order me around! I come and go as I please. It is entirely up to me. I would also like to tell you to leave a decent girl alone, because those who pay visits to a number of widows, and God knows who else, do not merit –"

"You liar!"

"If I am a liar, those who know you … are not!" Marin laughed.

"Even if I do, whose business is it? I can afford to go, because I am a man of means and I do not have to look after other people's sheep like you."

"It is better to look after other men's sheep than to go chasing after other men's wives."

"I dare you to say it once again!" yelled Mika in Marin's face.

"Ten times if I want to!"

Mika brandished his birch but Marin caught it and broke it.

A stern voice was heard behind their backs.

"What is going on?"

Mika turned round, rubbed his forehead and when he caught sight of Shana's mother, he laughed.

"Look, he's come to be your son-in-law!"

"He, to be my son-in-law? Never, as long as I live and as long as I am her mother! I did not nurture her and nourish her and care for her to give her finally to a beggar."

Then she looked at Marin and showed him the exit.

"Get out of my garden and do not come here again! Get lost and get yourself a girl more of your standing. Leave my Shana alone."

Marin bowed his head, looked at Shana wistfully, turned round and went slowly towards the exit. The sneering and acerbic laughter of Mika Balazhevich followed him along with the angry cursing of Shana's mother, who grabbed her daughter's hand and dragged her roughly into the yard.

In another yard a dog could be heard barking furiously, clanging the chain that tied it. A cart passed below the garden and from another garden a girl's singing could be heard:

"I love my beloved, my beloved loves me,

I hope women's tongues will not tear us free!"

The voice faded away through the open fields, above which the sun blazed like flames.

Chapter 3

On Saturday, in the early evening, Shana's father, Joza, entered the village pub and sat at a nearby table. The light of a paraffin lamp fell on the bare tables, on the small but corpulent figure of Joza Martich, and on the faded pictures hanging on the wall that had been there God only knows for how long. Joza was the only one in the pub and he ordered a glass of wine. At home in his cellar he had several large barrels of good old wine from his vineyards, far too many for him and his household, but in spite of this he liked to pay a visit to the pub that he was accustomed to from his bachelor days. Here, he and his company would usually meet, talking about news, playing cards, and drinking; and so the time passed more pleasantly. He was used to discussing the prices of the farm produce with the publican. He would also make plans about buying another acre of land that year, hoping the borough would not impose such a large tax on it, as if they were treating the people as infidels and not Christian souls. The publican himself sat at a table.

"Well, how should I put it, your Shana will be getting married this autumn!"

Joza twirled his moustache and stroked his beard.

"It is time for her. It is not as if she could not have married before, she has had suitors, but why should I give her away to a house that does not suit me? Anyway, she is still young, she is in no hurry and suitors like these will always be around. She does not need to be afraid of remaining a spinster."

"What you have just said is true, only I've heard that Mika will marry her," replied the publican.

"Well, to be honest, I am not overly bothered about it, but I can also tell you that I have nothing against him. I lived in great harmony with his late father and we were childhood friends. It is a pity that a man like him died."

"And he would be quite suitable for your Shana. You know, he is well off, he is rich."

"Anyway, we will see," replied Joza.

"I hear that he visits Shana," commented the publican.

"He is young and why not? I used to go visiting when I was young."

When Joza finished his glass, and as there was nobody else to talk to and he did not feel like talking to the pub-owner any longer, he left and went home. On the corner he met Mika.

"Oh, and where are you going?" he said, as if surprised, offering his hand.

"Just going to the village for a while."

"Have you been to our house perhaps?" asked Joza.

"I have, but now I won't!" replied Mika.

"*What?*" Joza was startled and, looking at him in shock, he asked: "And what is it that you do not like in my house?"

"Since Shana loves somebody else and does not want me, why should I go there?"

"And who told you that?"

"I have seen it for myself, nobody needs to tell me. Well, what can you do, Marin is a better suitor than me!"

Joza's face reddened deeply and his eyes blazed with fury.

"Haven't I told you that I forbade her to even speak with him? Have I not promised you that she will be yours?"

"You have promised indeed, I cannot say you have not, but you offered twenty acres of land for her, and to tell the truth I can get better than that with another."

"Who?" asked Joza.

"Well, recently they offered me a woman from a village with her thirty acres, but I prefer to marry Shana even if she would bring me twenty-five acres, because the land is close to mine and it could even be joined to mine, but now it looks as if nothing will come of it."

"I have promised you twenty acres and I will give you twenty acres. And you must admit that Shana is one in a million. She has no rival anywhere in beauty. Well, what more could you want? Do you not like her?"

"I am not saying I do not like her, but you are offering me too little for her."

"How much would you want?" asked Joza.

"Well, give me twenty-five and the deal is done!"

Joza scratched the back of his neck and paused to think. Twenty-five seemed too much to him. He thought it was a lot, but Mika also had forty acres and he could find a rich woman. If he did not give it to him, all the plans concerning Shana's marriage would come to nought.

"But why are we discussing this in the street? Come tomorrow in the afternoon to my house, I will be alone at home. The wife will go to church and then we can talk sensibly about it."

On his way home Joza thought that it would be best to give her to Mika, if only he did not ask for those five extra acres. But if Mika did not change his mind, he would talk to his wife and see what happened. And then, with Mika's father dead and Mika still young, only thirty, Joza might be able to take charge of Mika's farm as well.

He would not let go of Mika just like that, because Mika was a suitor without rival in this village. He could not bear to give his child to another village. He also hoped that Mika would not let go of Shana quite so easily and that he cared for her. He noticed how Mika looked at Shana and how his eyes filled with softness at her beauty.

Pondering on all these things, Joza came home and, having closed the door of the room behind him, he saw Shana sitting at the table. Her head was bowed with her hands in her lap, and her mother before her kept angrily turning round.

"What is up now?" asked Joza and threw his cap onto the bed.

"Indeed, you may ask," Shana's mother, Marta, yelled whilst strutting around in circles. "It would be better if I did not tell you!"

Joza stared at Marta and then at Shana.

"What has happened again?"

"I no longer know what to do with this girl! Has she gone mad, what is the matter with her? My sensible advice is wasted on her, my warnings, my gentle words too, everything is wasted on her; as if she were mad, as if she were possessed. If it goes on like this, I will not stay here. I would rather walk out and leave my own home, just to avoid being here and witnessing and listening to this disgrace."

"What disgrace? Tell me what happened!" shouted Joza angrily, coming closer to the table. "I cannot bear to have my honourable house disgraced. You have to remember this. So tell me what happened!"

"She does not want to forget that beggar. Just imagine what I heard two days ago! I cannot believe my own ears. When I left the house the other day, she met him in the garden. I heard it on my way, in the street, that he was with her. Does this become her? Has she been reduced to Marin? And who is he and what is he? Is he a suitable young man for her? Is he suitable for our well-to-do house? She is a disgrace to me and to you. I cannot go to church without people talking, whispering. And do I not know what they are saying and whispering? They are laughing at me behind my back, deriding us for having such a silly daughter."

Joza's face darkened and his eyes blazed with anger beneath his thick eyebrows. He stood before Shana, and, clenching his fists, he banged the table so hard that all the plates and glasses started rattling and dancing. "Have I not already told you to give him up? Do you think that you can bring disgrace on me?"

Shana was quietly wiping her tears with the edge of her apron. Marta was wiping the table with a cloth. Joza continued to shout angrily.

"This must be the last time! You had better remember this well! If I hear just once more that you are meeting with him, then you must be aware of the consequences. You are not a little girl without brains, who cannot think. You are a young woman ready for marriage and you cannot indulge in a young girl's daydreaming. I have found you a handsome and smart man, the best in the village."

"Well, what a handsome young man you *have* found for me!" Shana said, raising her eyes.

Joza was surprised and, turning round, he looked at Marta, as if seeking some sort of explanation. "And what is wrong with Mika? Any other girl would hardly be able to contain herself, if he looked her way. She would thank God and hold her head high, so that the whole village would envy her. And he is not good for you?"

Shana felt rage rising in her, her heart anguished; and she felt something heavy settling within her, threatening to rise and burst upwards, seeking release.

Then she suddenly jumped up and, holding her head high, she looked at her father and mother and said:

"I have been telling you to leave me alone, to stop torturing me every day. I do not want to see him, I do not want to hear of Mika, I want him out of my sight!"

She went to the next room slamming the door angrily behind her, so that Joza and Marta looked at each other in surprise and shook their heads distrustingly.

Marta sat on a chair. Joza filled his pipe. A large white cat was snoozing on a bench in the corner. A clock on the wall with long weights was ticking away slowly and ponderously.

Joza lit the tobacco in his pipe, and then he too sat down at the table and stared before him.

"She will come to her senses by this autumn," said Joza, mainly to himself.

"She is stubborn," added Marta.

"It will pass."

"Yes, it will pass, but if she sticks to her own way, what will I do with her? I have spoken to her so many times but what good has it done? She does not want to know. I have gone so far as to beat her several times, but it has made no difference."

"Try again in a gentler way, perhaps that will help. Go and see Godmother Manda. You are women, I can't teach you anything here. This is not my job."

"I will go tomorrow when I go to Vespers," decided Marta.

Joza was blowing out thick smoke, preoccupied with his own thoughts.

"Indeed, the other day I went to the fields and had a look at the position of Mika's fields. That part of land from the stream up to the top I would want to buy from Djuro Matin, so I would be able to join my land to Mika's. I could even raise a small farmstead there."

"Do whatever you think best," his wife replied.

"Mika has good horses."

"And his vineyards are beautiful."

"The only snag is that I can't strike a bargain with him. He wants five more acres of land; he is not satisfied with twenty. But I keep thinking twenty-five is a lot. Woman, it is a lot."

"When did he say this to you?"

"Today."

"And he will not change his mind?"

"Well, we shall see. I will speak to him. I wouldn't want to give away the lands along the dyke. They are good first-class soil."

"Offer him something else."

"Something else? Hmm, hmm. I will see."

"You must not let him slip through your fingers, even if you have to give an acre more, because such a son-in-law you will not find here again. And I will take care of Shana, I will try to persuade her, I will bring her to her senses somehow!"

On the bench the tomcat stretched his paws, his whiskers bristling. Opening wide his pale eyes, he jumped down onto the ground and slowly walked under the table. The hens screeched in the yard, a dog barked and the semi-dark shadows slipped through the window into the room, heralding an immediate need for candles.

Chapter 4

Marin opened the door and appeared in the kitchen. His nostrils were greeted by the smell that infused the kitchen from the pan in which his mother was cooking chicken.

"Praise be to Jesus!" he said, and leant on the doorpost.

"Forever amen!" answered his mother and faced him. She wiped her hands on her apron; tidied her headscarf; and smiling, she came close to Marin.

"Go on, take this off, sit down and have a rest, you must be tired. The supper will be ready any minute, I will just put another piece of wood on the fire."

She went to the firewood basket, put two or three pieces on the fire and then took Marin's cloak, putting it away in the cloakroom. Marin followed her out and went to check the vine that was at the end of the house, climbing up to the eaves.

It had been planted by his late father, when Marin was still a little boy, and now it had grown and climbed right under the eaves, and it bore fruit every year. The grapes were black and firm and they exuded the scent of sweet young wine. As he looked at the grapevine, his mother came up and stood behind him:

"Thank God, it is good, there will be grapes this year too, just like last year."

"I will have to tie this bit here, because I would like it to grow this way, so that it will provide some lovely shade."

His mother watched him tie up one end of the vine so that it could grow in a semi-arch, and then she came closer and said rather sadly:

"Oh, my son, how this vine has grown. I remember it as if it were now, when your father planted it. Oh, how quickly the years have passed. Who would have known ... You were a child then, running after me, and now, look, you are a grown young man. And I will tell you how I feel now and what thoughts come into my head. When you go to the fields or go with the sheep and I remain alone here, I go into the yard, I come here and I look around, oh, my Lord, and I keep thinking that it would be good if you were to get married, so that I would not be alone in the house. You know, I walk around and I can already see your children following me about, I can see myself picking grapes for them, putting them into their baskets and getting them ready for school. And it makes me feel so good, I rejoice, and it is lovely to go on living. But when I see that there is nobody around, I bow my head, my heart becomes heavy, I feel sad and often a tear trickles down my cheek. You know I would just like to see you married and for me to have a grandson, and then I would not mind dying."

Marin looked at the vine whilst his mother spoke, then, bending his head, he smiled quietly and painfully:

"Mama, everything at the right time."

"I find it hard to be alone in the house. Bring me someone so that I will not always be alone. During the day it is not so bad, but at night when you are not here, and I am enclosed in these four walls, I feel so miserable. I have nobody to talk to and there is nobody to talk to me."

Marin came close to his mother, took her by the hand and said: "I will bring you someone, don't worry, Mama."

She stroked his cheek and cheered up, already seeing her future daughter-in-law. In the room she placed the supper on the table. The paraffin lamp smouldered, casting a red light onto the table; onto beds; and, descending down to the ground, it stopped there in peace. Only from time to time would it play a little, swaying and then settling down again.

After supper Marin put a hat on and said to his mother that he was going out to see his friends in the village. The evening was tranquil and bright. The mulberry trees cast long shadows on walls, the path was moonlit, and the light of the candles poured out through the windows of some houses, falling on the path in front of them.

Marin dug his hands into his pockets, set his hat askew and quietly and tenderly sang to himself:

"If only those little roses knew

The grief of my heart,

They would shed a tear or two

To soothe my aching smart!"

Whilst whistling this song, he thought about the things that his mother spoke about. Her words would not leave him. He could see for himself that his mother was old, that it was hard for her to be alone in the house and that she needed a helping hand. It was not the first time she had spoken to him about this. It had happened several times before, but he used to console her by saying that he would get married, that he would find a girl. Then her face would light up, and her clasped hands would settle in her lap, and her eyes would look with great love and tenderness at Marin. And he would only bow his head and think his thoughts, which would often make him sad. He knew he could not remain as he was now, that he could not continue to leave his mother alone; but he also knew that he could not get married.

There was no shortage of girls who would gladly marry him. There were plenty; but as soon as he thought about marrying, his heart became heavy, his soul in agony, and he would wander far into the fields and carry on wandering until dark, returning home through the plum orchard and going to bed with a sense of loss. He felt that he could not marry anyone except Shana, because he would never be happy or content with another. The thought of Shana would always torture him, he would always feel depressed, he would feel humiliated, despised and belittled, because he was poor. He never spoke about Shana to his mother, not even in passing, because he was sure of the astonishment he would see in her face. Therefore, he carried his pain and his hope in his heart, as something sacred or precious, that he never wanted to entrust to anyone because he knew very well that people could be jealous and envious. But his heart ached when he saw his mother sitting in the corner or on the threshold, looking somewhere far away. Then she would not say anything, but her face revealed her thoughts very clearly and this silent pain, and the silent longing, pained him doubly. He wanted to help her as soon as possible, but he did not know how. And now, whilst he was thinking about it, from a distance, in the main street, he could hear the maidens' song. It was inspired by their enticing, all-consuming desires, hopes, restlessness and frolics, to the extent that it brought into the evening tranquillity the scent of blossoming youth and blossoming longings, burning in the voices and songs that flowed into the soft darkness and dissipated somewhere at the end of the village:

"*My beloved, build me a house with tiles,*

I like to stroll around in the nice palace.

My beloved is my darling

His raven-black eyes are roving.

Though a berry I may be, and my beloved a grape,

Still a grape a berry can drape!"

As soon as the female voices fell silent, as if enveloped by the falling dusk, the robust, full-throated, restless, confident and fresh young men's voices burst forth, rising powerfully high above the houses, much more powerfully than the female voices, suddenly filling the whole street and overflowing; and high above these voices, the voice of the leader quivered triumphantly:

"*When I stroll past your palace,*

Your heart shall all be a race.

The moon shining, a flower blooming,
What is my darling now doing?

My beloved, more precious than gold,
When in my arms I her enfold.

Her tiny teeth like tiny pearls
For my beloved, my heart yearns."

Marin stopped for a second, listening to the song. Then he turned the corner and met with his friends. When they saw him, they held out their hands, tapped him on the back with joy, shook hands and said to him:

"We began to think that you were ill, because you have not been here with us."

"I spend all my time with the sheep."

"Well, at least you could have come on Sundays to the circle-dancing. If you'd been with us last time, you'd have laughed your head off. We enjoyed ourselves so much. We got so drunk that we had to be carried home and the next day you should have seen how the women gossiped about us! How they examined us from our infancy to the present moment! But who cares, let them say what they like. Indeed, are we not young men?"

At the end of the street they met the girls approaching them. These fell silent when the young men came closer. Each had his own girl, each hastened to his own, only Marin remained staring at them. He saw them joyful, mischievous and happy, and his heart felt heavy. He leant against a wall at the side and stared down the street. Each man disappeared with his own girl, joyful that he could be with the girl close to his heart.

Marin wanted to walk along any other street so that he did not have to stand there, but somebody approached him from behind, placing hands on his eyes, waiting for him to guess who it was.

He gently removed the hands from his eyes and, turning around, said:

"Stana, where did you spring from?"

"Did you not see me?"

"No."

"I noticed you immediately and I recognised you from afar. Will you come to the circle-dance tomorrow?"

Marin thought for a moment, and then a smile touched the edge of his lips:

"Why not indeed?"

"It will make me happy. Tell Marko to come too. You know, I can tell you, although I could not tell another soul: Marko has been avoiding me and I do not know why. Everything was good and wonderful between us and now suddenly he has changed."

"Marko?" exclaimed Marin in surprise.

"You know, I have heard that they are forcing him to take Olga Mijich."

"It can't be!"

"I did not think it was possible, but now I am beginning to believe it. Last time he danced almost the whole evening with her, he kept her company and I felt like sinking into the ground. The women immediately started gossiping and they did not spare me in the least. I went home alone and wept. Please, tell him, or ask him about me, but in such a way that he would not know it was coming from me."

"I will tell him. I am sure this was a joke and that he just wanted to tease you a little."

"I do not know what he wanted, but I am afraid and my heart feels heavy. And it was so wonderful until Olga started interfering. Since she stepped in, everything has gone bad."

Marin walked beside her silently with a bowed head. Peace descended upon the low white houses, lulling them to slumber. The moon stood high above the cemetery. Somewhere a door opened and closed, and a draw-well's sweep squeaked.

Marin listened to the muffled sounds of the evening and then he looked at Stana:

"And what about Shana? Have you seen her?"

Stana placed her hand on his arm and paused:

"I have seen her."

"When?"

"She told me that Mika came a few times and gave her an apple. He was ingratiating himself with her. Can you imagine, he told her that he loved her and that he could not live without her any longer. God knows what else he told her. She left him there and went out of her house. He watched her go and swore to himself: 'Out of pure spite you will be mine. Since you are stubborn, Mika will show you what he is made of and what he can do. And I will break Marin's ribs so he will know how to keep out of other people's affairs.'"

Marin looked grim. He clenched his fists.

"He had better leave me alone, because no good will come of it. There are limits!"

"Shana asked me to give you her greetings and she said that she would come to the circle-dance tomorrow. You must be there. She would like to speak with you. She said you really had to come."

Marin wiped his forehead with his hand and after a short pause, he said:

"I will come. Tell her that I will come. Give her my greetings."

When Stana entered her yard, he walked on, thinking. He turned around the corner, having decided to walk past Shana's house. Above the village the moon kept watch and the stars were very bright. From time to time, the voices of young men and women could be heard singing from the top of the village. Shana's windows were dark and there were no lights in the whole of the house.

He stopped for a moment and watched the windows. "I am sure she must be asleep now and has no idea that I am here thinking of her. I wonder what she is dreaming about, what fills her thoughts on waking."

When he came close to his house he noticed the lights. He knew that his mother was still sitting on the bench and waiting for him. Once again he turned around and cast a look at Shana's house, and then he opened the gate and entered the yard. At this moment his mother blew the candle out. He went to the bedroom and, once in bed, he placed his hands under his head, surrendering to his thoughts and feelings.

Chapter 5

On Sunday afternoon, as promised, Mika Balazhevich came to visit Joza. He wore a new, well-brushed black hat and, on his feet, highly polished boots. A thick gold chain hung on his shirt across his waistcoat. With a handkerchief tucked in the pocket of his black jacket, Mika looked a real dandy. When added to this the trimmed moustache, carefully combed hair and the perfumed face, then it is no surprise that many a widow sighed over him and followed him with her gaze from across the fence. He did not easily reject their sighs and so stories circulated, which, in the eyes of the more sober and serious people, aroused suspicions and bad impressions.

When Mika entered the room, Joza had his glasses on and a pencil in his hand with a piece of paper before him. The paper was full of calculations that Joza had been occupied with since lunchtime.

When he saw Mika, he raised his head, peered at him over his glasses, placed the pencil onto the paper and, smiling kindly, got up and shook hands with him, saying:

"I have just been working out how much the land would cost me if I tilled it myself. Of course I cannot do it all by myself, but I was working out how it would be if I dismissed farm labourers and occasional workers. Or if I organised it somehow to give them less. They will just have to be satisfied with what I give them, because they have to know that jobs are scarce anyway."

Mika drew the chair up and sat at the table.

"Anyway, I cannot stand some of the occasional labourers any longer," Joza said as he went into the other room, whence he brought back a full bottle of wine and two glasses. Placing the bottle and the glasses on the table, he continued:

"I can't stand people like Ivan Zhivkovich and he will be the first I get rid of."

Joza poured wine into the glasses. Then he raised his glass of wine towards the light and, looking at it, he said with enthusiasm:

"Look at it, this is real wine!"

Clinking their glasses, they drank.

"It is good! Quite good. It has an excellent aroma and it is smooth," said Mika, placing the glass on the table and turning towards Joza.

"And how many barrels have you got?"

"I have three more of this kind. I am keeping them for Shana's wedding, but I have some more, a bit younger, seven barrels. I was asked to sell them, but I did not wish to sell at the present price. I was not offered enough. I will wait for the price to go up and anyway I am in no hurry."

"I have sold mine and I now regret it, because I've heard that the price will go up. My mother kept telling me to be patient and wait, but I could not be bothered. Well, what can you do, you are never sensible enough and you live and learn."

"You are right there," accepted Joza. "But I will certainly get rid of that Ivan as soon as possible."

"What has he done to you?"

"He is mean as hell. Well, what do you know, he cheats me at every step. Even when I visit him at his home, he never offers me anything, only water is ever on the table. I am even used to eating in my occasional workers' homes because I think that they also eat of the crops that grow on my land."

Joza again raised his glass, clinking his with Mika's. Then, looking Mika straight in the eye, he said:

"You see, whenever you visit me, you shall have everything in the house and you shall never want for anything. My house is the first in the village and does not need to be ashamed of any other. And the land I am giving you is fertile, first class, you will not find better. Now I have sown the wheat and look how tall it is already."

"Could you not give me that acre along the embankment? True, it is a bit wet at times, but it would be really useful to me."

"That one, no, but let us say the land right up close to the dyke."

"Close to the dyke?" Mika was thinking.

"Immediately next to the dyke," said Joza.

"But there it is always wet and waterlogged."

"I do not deny it, but you will always have good reeds. And reeds have a good price now. Every year they are sought after by the neighbouring villages. They were here last Sunday too, you must know that yourself, I do not need to tell you! The whole village knows about it."

"Why don't you keep that and sell it yourself?" said Mika.

Joza scratched the back of his neck. He took the glass in his hands and, twisting it, he said:

"I do not need the reeds now. I thought you would find them useful. I know you do not know how this land lies, it has been a long time since you have been there, so why don't we go now and take a look?"

Mika paused to think: "Shall we go now?"

"Tomorrow I will not have time. It is a working day and I have a lot of work to do. You will see the land and you will like it. Because it is best to see it for yourself."

"Then I have to go home first to change, because my suit and my boots will get dirty."

"Yes, you do that. I will also get ready."

Mika got up.

Joza poured some more wine into the glasses, looked at Mika knowingly, winked at him and said:

"To your health! There is more where this came from!"

As soon as Mika left, Joza looked at the bottle and frowned and shook his head:

"This one doesn't half drink, he does not seem to know when to stop. He does not care that in somebody else's house he should not drink as much as he wants."

He was about to pour himself another glass when Martin Pavich entered, looking all done in.

"If you have a heart, help!" he said, whilst still at the door, taking his cap off and holding it in his hand.

Joza placed the bottle on the table. He stared at Martin and scowled. But quickly, as if he remembered something, his face was lit by a smile, his moustache twitched and he came over to Martin.

"What good brings you here? Do sit down, why are you standing there?"

Martin looking down at the cap in his hands, and bending even lower, his eyes blazing, his hair falling untidily over his forehead, said:

"It is trouble, indeed, trouble that brings me here."

"But what sort of trouble could have befallen you?"

"You know it very well yourself, I do not need to tell you! You should not have done this to a poor man. You could have waited a bit longer, I would have got the money and somehow repaid you. If you had waited until after the harvest, I could have earned a bit of money and then paid my debt. Now at the worst time you placed me in the hands of the lawyer. How can I repay you at this time? It is impossible now. I cannot leave my children to starve and weep. Also, I am sure that you do not need the money so desperately that you could not wait a while. That is why I came to beg you to spare me not ruin me, as I am a poor man, because everything depends on you. Can you imagine where I would go if my house were sold in a week's time? If the lawyer sold it, where I would find a roof over my head, where I would put my children. If I were on my own, with nobody to care for, I could manage somehow to feed myself, but there are my children, my wife and my old mother too. I cannot take them out onto the streets!"

Whilst Martin was speaking, Joza kept scratching and stroking his beard, now looking at him, now at the ground. Then he raised his head.

"You know yourself, it has been a while now, and you have not repaid my money. I cannot give my money to all and sundry. I need it myself. I did not find this money under a bush either. I have sweated blood for it and worked very hard. And I had to put the case into the lawyer's hands or I would have waited forever. You are not even paying the interest, never mind the capital, and what else could I have done, but place you in the lawyer's hands?"

"How could I start paying you the capital when I am paying you the interest at twenty-five percent? And you have already taken this. Indeed, it is rather a lot."

"Well, if it had been a lot, you should not have agreed to it. I did not force you to borrow money from me. Of course not. It is not my fault. You agreed to the interest and so you should repay honestly, because I gave you the money treating you as an honest man. You have to admit that yourself, because had it not been like that, I would never have given the money to you. Have I not said, 'Martin, repay my money if you do not want to be handed over to the lawyer'?"

"You did say."

"And you said: 'I cannot.'"

"Indeed, I cannot."

"Well then, what else could I have done? I placed it in the lawyer's hands and let him deal with it."

"And he dealt me a sale of the house over my head. And I can go to God knows where. Will you receive me to avoid us perishing on the streets?"

Joza became thoughtful. Silence descended on the room.

"Listen!" said Joza after a brief moment, looking at Martin. "So that you could not say that I refused to help you, I will do this out of love for you. So, listen! There is no way that you could repay me the money?"

"How could I?" Martin raised his arms wide. "No, I cannot."

"All right. The house will be sold; the lawyer has taken care of it. He has done a good job! And it is usually for a pittance in such cases. I am sure that it will be bought by that tradesman, Schneider."

"I have heard that he is already enquiring ..." said Martin.

"So you can see, I do not wish for your house to be sold to someone else. I could never do such a thing. God forbid, that I would not help a poor man. I lent you the money last time."

Martin smiled grudgingly and shook his head.

"And here I think," continued Joza, "as two honest people we could come to an agreement."

"How do you mean?" asked Martin.

"How? Here is how. You will make your house over to me for the debt, because it is better for you to give it to me than to that German, and I will permit you to go on living in it and you will pay me the rent. There, I will do this out of love for you, I would not do it for anybody else."

"I would pay the rent in my own house?"

Martin expressed his surprise and looked at him timidly, as if he could not believe what he was hearing. Suddenly everything went dark before his eyes, unsteady, as if he were about to fall into an abyss, standing on its very edge, holding his head in despair! That he should give him the house and pay him the rent as well! That he should give him the house he worked so hard to acquire, for which he spent many nights without sleep in order to leave something to his children! To give it to Joza for a pittance now and to pay him the rent for it as well for the privilege to live in it!

"No, never!" A dark voice screamed inside him and a cloud enveloped his thoughts. He felt as if something was breaking in his soul, he felt as if he were going to sob for the bitterness that was threatening to break out of him. With his bare hands he wanted to pulp this good-for-nothing loan shark who stood before him, looking at him with his blinking, sly and feverish eyes, as if to mock him as well. And this loan shark considered it some sort of kindness, whilst all the time it was his intention to gain this poor man's house. This is why he had placed him in the hands of the lawyer.

"No, you will never have it, I would rather the German bought it, but I will not give it to you!" Martin yelled full of rage, and moved towards the door.

"Then the German will certainly buy it!"

"But it will not be yours!"

"We will see about that too!"

Martin turned round and stood stock-still; nobody could have budged him from that place:

"Watch out, be careful, if my house were sold, I would have nothing else to lose! This could become far too dear for you. Remember, that which is earned with toil and blood, would be paid for with blood!" Then he slammed the door behind him and left.

Joza watched him go and, shrugging his shoulders, said quite calmly: "Well, I wanted to help him, but if he refuses, I cannot force him. Since he wants his house sold, let it be sold. I will get my money and he can do what he likes, he will not be able to blame me. Had he repaid my money, I would not have handed him to the lawyer and the lawyer would not have been selling the house."

He went to the other room and changed his clothes. Then Mika arrived. They went to look at the land and they tried to come to an agreement. When they left the village, a great green plain opened before them and, above it, a peaceful blue sky. They took a narrow path between the brushwood leading them finally to a clearing, whence they climbed onto the embankment and gazed at the open fields, meadows and rich wheat-fields.

Then they descended to the valley and in a moment were hidden in the high reeds, which rustled after them as if bent by the wind during a storm. They came out at the dyke, the edge of which was covered with reeds and grass. Joza took off his hat, wiped his forehead with a handkerchief, and paused for breath. The swallows flew above, the smell of grass was in the air, the acacia trees were budding and beginning to turn green, the wheat stalks were erect, and the plain was undulating in the light breeze, whilst a new and nervous life was burgeoning from within the bosom of the earth.

Joza took a few deep breaths of air into his lungs, and for a moment he listened to the soundless hum of life which secretly smouldered through the grass, the acacia trees and the young willows. Then he gazed across the wheat fields and his gaze stopped at the piece of land, where the reeds grew thick and uncut.

"There, I will give you this!"

He raised his arm, pointing at the plain. Then he took a few steps, stopped, and, pulling out a handful of the grass, looked at it.

Mika looked down and, nodding his head unhappily, said:

"It is not much use."

"If you work to make the land less wet, you will be able to cut the reed and plough the rest. And in a year or two it will be fertile. You will only need to manure it. The soil must never be neglected."

Mika raised his arm:

"And whose meadow is that?"

"Stipich's."

"Ah, yes, I know."

"He has sown grass, but it is somewhat poor."

They had a look at one part and now they went along the dyke to look at the other. Mika saw immediately that the soil was not good and thought that this was the reason why Joza wanted to give it to him. He had already decided to ask for the piece where the wheat was growing, but it was on the other side of the embankment.

As soon as he voiced his request, Joza shrugged his shoulders, raised his hat higher off his forehead and said:

"That I cannot give you."

"And this I do not want. The soil is bad. Very bad. I will have practically no use for it."

Joza paused again and thought. He was thinking of a plan to please Mika somehow. If he did not want to accept what he offered, he would have to think of something better.

Finally Joza said: "Do you not like this piece?"

"No."

"Hmm ... All right, I will give you two acres on the other side of the embankment, but in return you will plough the piece of land below the village every year free of charge."

"Two acres?" Mika placed his finger over his mouth and lifted his head. "Two acres?" he repeated, and walked on a few steps. "Two more and we can shake hands!"

"I will give you two, but no more. Those twenty plus these two, that's enough. Two more, and let's shake hands."

They faced each other. Their eyes met. They were silent. The wind was blowing in the reeds. A sparrow flew past them. Mika took another few steps and then turned round and came back:

"'Two more and here is my hand.'"

Joza looked down on the ground, thinking. Then he crossed his arms at his back and went towards the embankment.

"Two more, two more," Joza kept repeating, as he climbed up onto the embankment. "Hmm, hmm, we will see, I will speak with the wife."

They climbed up onto the embankment and descended to the part of the land that was sown with wheat. Behind them only the imprints of their footsteps were left in the grass. In the distance a dark veil began to cover the sky, becoming bigger and bigger; it then stood still in one place for a long time. The whole plain rested calmly in the balmy slumber; only the birds flew around, rising into the sky, now descending onto a branch, now into the wheat. If either man had looked back towards the village, he would have seen a slim white steeple rising above the white houses, as if watching over everyone, as if showing all of us that time passes over us and over our wishes, and that it will take us with it. But neither of these men seemed to be aware of it in that moment.

Chapter 6

As soon as Shana returned from Vespers with her mother, she changed the clothes she had worn to church and put on the clothes she usually wore to the circle-dance on Sunday evenings. Her friend Stana had already told her in the church during Vespers that she would pick her up as soon as she had changed and had had a bite to eat, and that then they would go together to the dance. Shana was putting her Sunday clothes into a large open chest, when her mother came in and stood behind her.

"Will you have supper first and then go?" asked Marta, holding her prayer book in her hand. Over her arm she had a small cloth used for kneeling on the church's stone floor.

Shana faced her, thinking.

"I will eat and then that's over and done with," she said, and, closing the chest, she went to the next room.

Whilst she was getting ready, her thoughts were of Marin. She felt both tenderness and a certain unease. She felt joyful at the thought of being next to him again in the circle-dance, happy to know that he would certainly dance beside her. She already felt a warm glow from inside rising to her cheeks and making her blush, and she felt a thrill at the thought of their hands holding tight and not letting go, her eyes burning as if on fire. But she also felt uneasy at the thought of the women, stealthily observing her every gaze and her every movement so they could interpret these tomorrow amongst themselves, mercilessly judging everything they had seen and concluded.

She disliked those women because they poked their noses into everybody's business. With their tongues they would marry and wed, thus making themselves the judges of public opinion in the village. Woe betide those who ran foul of them, because they had no pity. But these thoughts were immediately supplanted by new, fresh thoughts of this evening and the joy before her. Her days seemed very long when she did not leave the house at all, and was busy with tidying the rooms.

For her, Sunday was a real feast day because it meant a rest and going to the circle-dance with her friends. As she was getting ready, the sunshine poured in through the window, but already tinged with red, flowing over the plant pots on the windowsill, holding the flowers that had been planted in them. Then it reached the wardrobe, touching the apples and pears intended for the sick in the house, should there unfortunately be a sick person found within. As Shana put a hairpin in to fix her hair, she heard the street door open and then the joyful and carefree voice of a young maiden laughing and talking. Shana quickly left the mirror, threw her colourful shawl over her shoulders and went into the kitchen.

"Here we are, we are ready to go!" her friends said.

"Do sit down for a moment!" insisted Marta, who suddenly found herself there.

"Why should we sit down? We have not tired ourselves yet."

"Just a little while, so we can 'sleep' better."

The girls sat down and Shana offered them the pie that had been made on the day. Shana had already had a quick bite on her own because Marta had said she was not hungry yet and would eat when Joza returned from the village. As they turned to leave the room, Marta stopped Shana and said to her on her own:

"Be careful, I do not want to hear things tomorrow."

"Of course, I heard you!" answered Shana, without really listening.

"Do not even look at him! Why should you care, you know he is not for you."

"Of course, of course, I already heard you!" Shana said quickly at the exit and ran after her friends, who were already waiting for her in the street.

Whilst walking in the street towards the circle-dance, they saw wives in front of the houses, sitting either on benches or small chairs or on the blankets that were spread on the ground. Some distance away, men played cards and talked about the most recent news or about their experiences when they had served in the Great War. But many turned their talk to the present difficult times, to the great crisis, to unemployment and no earnings. They complained that, in spite of all that, the local borough imposed heavy taxes, which with the best will in the world they could not pay.

When the maidens walked past the women, the women would say:

"How pretty you made yourselves look?"

"Indeed!"

"But go on, quickly, the music is playing! You must not be late, they are sure to be waiting."

"Well, those who love us will certainly wait!" responded the maidens jokingly.

Men would usually glance from their cards, wink and add:

"Look, look! How shy they are and blushing. We also keep some red paper on the beams and we will give you some to redden your cheeks!"

"You leave it where it is and keep it for your wives to beautify themselves!"

All this banter was usually accompanied by laughter. The girls were used to such remarks and they could never make them angry. Just as the remarks were meted out of habit in quick banter, so they were forgotten just as quickly.

From further on, the sounds of music could already be heard. The big bass that Djuka Sejin was playing could be heard far away, a sound that was somewhat heavy and soft and rolled down the street, and it alone rumbled into the distance. When the girls approached, the high and penetrating sounds of a violin and tamburitza could be heard and the yard was resounding with music. The young men were already caught up in the circle, dancing with their narrow-brimmed hats askew, and the maidens darting glances at them in order to spot their beloved ones, whilst the women were shoving on their thresholds where they were higher up in order to get a better view of the circle. Some of them were also underneath the morello cherry near where the dancing was usually held. The musicians would stand in the middle and the dancing went on around them. As the night fell, flooding the yard with its scents and soft shadows, the atmosphere became more lively and joyous. It seemed that all this was growing out of the darkness, turning round and round in the shadows, absorbing itself into them, and then freeing itself as in a dream.

Shana joined the circle, raised her head and waited to catch a glimpse of Marin from somewhere. The violin was sobbing so wantonly, weeping, then abating with melancholy, and everyone was carried by the wave of the music, as if all feet were dancing by themselves. The accompaniment that filled the sound of the violin gave it an exalted feeling, penetrating boldly into people's chests, intoxicating them with its sound ...

The large and colourful circle was swaying. Then arose the high, trembling, somewhat painful voice of a maiden, and it vibrated in the sounds of the music above them somewhere far away in a sigh, in darkness, as if it longed for the heights:

"*Dancing in the circle, such a great fun,*

No room for you, my dear old bun.

Brilliant star, what says you in the sky,

My beloved, slighting me, for worse?

My beloved, do not tie your horse,

My own kin know you haven't got a penny."

Her voice was soaring high, hearts were soaring high and the music was tearing at everyone's thoughts and feelings. When this voice fell silent, a new voice, robust and masculine, was heard, as if bursting out from the earth and then so raw and ponderous, but in spite of that, somehow gentle and pleasant, pouring out and filling all the empty spaces within the circle:

"*He loves his beloved in the plum orchard,*

as not even flowers love me in my closet ...

My boots, my shiny uppers,

Only bait for the nutters.

All of them with gall will I fill,

Only my beloved with sugar and thrill."

The circle was swaying wildly now, feet skipping, tangling, heels tapping, floating above the trodden ground and dancing to the rhythm of the musicians.

From the sidelines, women craned their necks, pushed with their elbows, and raised themselves on tiptoes in order to have a better view. It was getting darker and darker. The paraffin lamps were brought out and hung up high on the wall above the entrance door so that the light fell on the yard. In the street, there was a lot of running, shouting and squealing. These were the children racing around, scuffling, and rolling on the ground.

Suddenly Shana caught sight of Marin standing by the house entrance. Her heart trembled with a vague fear. He was there, her heart pounding, she closed her eyes, her hands tightly clenched, she felt as if she were sinking. She no longer paid any attention to anyone in the circle. Everything disappeared before his figure, only the music tore at her feelings mercilessly and carried her high on its wings. But he stood still at the door, pensively watching the circle. She felt his gaze resting on her, following her and staying with her. She lowered her eyes but they involuntarily sought the figure by the door. She wanted him to come, to dance beside her in spite of all the women gawking. But he stood still and did not move. His gaze was directed at her and she felt its power. And then suddenly, as if awakening from a dream, he pushed his way through the crowd, eyed the dancing circle and caught up with Shana.

She merely trembled, but in her inner self she felt a warm thrill that reached the tips of her fingers. Then, the musicians stopped playing and in a flash a silence descended on the yard, the only noise coming now from the unruly children in the street, who would never leave anyone in peace. The maidens linked arms and in groups went out into the street to take a walk for a while, and a breather.

Shana took Marin's hand. They went out into the street alone. The women were pushing and craning their necks and making comments amongst themselves. The musicians were tuning their tamburitzas.

Out in the street Marin stopped and addressed Shana.

"I cannot go on like this, I cannot bear it any longer."

"I cannot either. I am afraid."

"Have they been talking to you again?"

"Need you ask? They do not leave me alone even for a moment. I have already gone mad, out of my mind. They will force me to marry Mika and I cannot do it."

"Force you?" repeated Marin, smiling wryly. "Why would they force you to marry?"

"Because they say that he is the young man for me, that he is rich! And that is that!"

"And what did you say?"

"I will not, I will not!"

"Oh, Shana!" He squeezed her hand, looking into her eyes.

"Today we have to come to an agreement as to what to do. I would rather do anything than marry Mika. He disgusts me. I can't stand the sight of him. Today, Father and Mika were again arranging details. They also went to look at the land."

"Shana, do you really love me?"

She pulled away, looking surprised at this question:

"Why do you ask?"

"Could you make a sacrifice for me?"

"Where do these questions come from? Do you doubt me? Are you not convinced by now that I love you and that I want *you*, alone; that I cannot bear anybody else? You make me sad."

Marin took her hands:

"Do not be angry. I am glad and I believe you. I am asking because I am afraid for you when they all go on the attack, when they all conspire to tear you away from me and persuade you at all costs to marry Mika. As you can see, Shana, your parents do not care for me. They do not care for me and you know that I have never harmed them in any way. I have never harmed them in any way and they hate me now. I know why they hate me! Oh, I know very well why. Well, they hate me only because I love you and I am poor, I am not rich like Mika. I know that if I were as rich as him, they would care for me, they would open their door wide to me and they would receive me as they receive him now. Yes, I know this, Shana! See, I am guilty because I am poor."

The evening was getting darker. The stars began appearing in the vault of the heavens. The street had a fresh scent. The two of them fell silent. From the yard could be heard babbling, exclamations, young men singing, children crying, and women calling.

Shana sighed.

"And that is why I have waited for you so impatiently tonight in order to see you and to talk to you. So that I would know what we should do. I know I have to be obedient to them, because they are my parents, because they brought me up, they raised me, they gave me life, but I cannot do what my heart cannot bear."

Marin stared into the street, pondering:

"You know what? Tomorrow I will inform you through Marko what we are going to do. For some time I have been thinking, but I will think it over tonight and tomorrow, and I will let you know. Be ready."

Then the maidens came back. They returned to dancing. Music could be heard from the yard.

"Shana, let's go, they are playing!" her friends called.

"Just a moment, I am coming!"

Marin accompanied Shana to the circle and stood aside.

The circle began swaying. The air was filled with the warmth of the maidens' longings and the young men's gazes. Marin too felt the call from within, something warm and sweet, that could turn into something infinitely good, so that he felt like hugging everyone and shaking hands with everyone with inexpressible emotion.

"Oh, how everything would be wonderful if I were able to go and ask for Shana's hand from her parents! What a relief it would be, how wonderful life would be!"

And then he remembered his mother, he remembered that she needed things to change and some help. He would like to help her, but how could he?

He was deep in thought and before him the circle was swaying, the ground shaking under the feet of the skilled and tireless male and female dancers, whose foreheads were beaded with sweat but they did not care. Today they would have their heart's desire and tomorrow there would be time for resting. Then, a female voice was heard:

"My goodness – what can you do?

To forget my old love I cannot do!

My new love loves and fights,

To forget my old love it smarts."

The young men were stomping their heels, raising and lowering their heads rakishly, now to the left, now to the right. Their foreheads now scowling, now brightening, the eyes flashing restlessly in this rakish, foppish way, only to rest on the one who took their fancy, who gave them much joy and hope, but also much anxiety. A lot of sighing and hidden grief, but they do not betray themselves, they pretend that this is nothing to do with them. And only when they are alone, they run their hands through their hair, bow their heads or look into the distance, shaking their heads and sighing.

The women crowd more and more around Marin, their pupils dilated, clutching their shawls hastily thrown over their shoulders, rising on tiptoes and pushing each other. Near the wall of the house children were fighting, screaming, their voices bursting through the music, but nobody was listening to them, nobody was taking any notice of them. As they fought, so were they left to make up.

"Look, it is him!" commented the women, pushing and shoving.

"Who?" others asked.

"How well he's dressed himself up, like a gentleman."

"Where is he?"

"There, I am sure he will join the circle."

"I can't see him."

"I hope he will stand next to her."

"I hope so too."

"He knows a good thing when he sees it. She would not be the first to be taken in by him, she will not escape him either. And why is he not good enough for her? Because she has to entertain him? The greater the debauchee, the better. The debauchees provide like gentlemen because they can afford to, they can do it. Well, he who is without cannot, hard as he may try!"

Marin did not even bother to turn around. He watched the circle: Shana, to be precise. She certainly noticed it and felt it. The important thing for him was that she understood him; that she was with him and all the gossip behind him was of no consequence. Let them gossip. Today, this; tomorrow, something quite the opposite. Then he was startled. His face became attentive. He saw Mika nearing the circle, he saw him stop to see which girl to join. Marin couldn't take his eyes off him. He had never had a quarrel with him nor was he on friendly terms with him, but as long as he could remember, he had never liked him. Marin found him repulsive and that is why he despised him, more so since Mika was trying to win over Shana by coercion: from that point on, he could not even look at him. He was doubly repulsive to him now.

The violin strings were moaning painfully and intoxicatingly. The tamburitza's piercingly delicate sound was a bewitching wave that carried the circle dancers, their thoughts and hearts, while Mika stood and watched. Then he pushed forwards and, separating Shana's hand from her friend's hand, he caught up with her. Shana's face suddenly changed. She blushed from her cheekbones to her forehead and down to her small and beautifully curved chin. And Mika tilted his head, looked at her slyly, winked and started singing:

"I am a rake, a rich one too

to seduce a young maiden is easy to do!"

The circle was swaying and Shana's friend, knowing Mika's intentions and wanting to sting him, started a high-pitched song of her own:

"My joy, your eyes may a ray of sunshine be

all in vain, my heart cares not a hoot for thee!

If I marry you, fettered I should be,

a husband though you would be

a withered rose you shall have lived to see, ooh la la ...!"

Mika looked at her in askance and scowled. The circle-dance was whirling furiously. Shana let go and left the circle and stood aside. Mika turned white, he was shocked. His blood boiled in his veins. It seemed to him that she had given him a merciless slap in the face, that she had dishonoured him publicly. Mika was thinking to himself that she did not even want to dance next to him and she had shown this without hesitation. She had belittled him. This was terribly hurtful to him. The blood rushed to his head. His hands trembled and tightened, he scowled and his eyes darkened. How dare she disgrace him publicly: him, whom so far no woman had ever got the better of, never mind humiliated. How dare Shana humiliate him in front of everybody! No, he would not take this lying down.

As soon as the circle-dance stopped he went to seek her out. But she was not in the yard. Neither was Marin. It was clear to him that they were together again and he was not wrong. He found them in the dark, beneath a mulberry tree, standing there in silence. He approached them angrily and exasperated, and stood in front of Marin.

"You must stop this business, because it could cost you dearly!" he told Marin, piercing him with his eyes threateningly.

"What business?"

"You leave her alone!"

"And why should I leave her alone? Do you perhaps think that she is fonder of you than of me? And therefore I should leave her alone?"

"She is not for you."

"But she is for you?"

"Yes, she is for me, because I am a man and you are a beggar, not a man. And if I see you again with her, I will show you what Mika can do."

"What did you say?" At these words Marin trembled, shaking his fists.

"I said what I wanted to say! Get lost, away from her and I do not wish to see you!"

"Well, that is where you are wrong! Are you not ashamed of chasing a girl who does not care for you? Do you feel no shame in front of these decent people?"

"You, a beggar, should be ashamed of trying to improve your standing."

"I may be poor, but I am honest and not a scoundrel like you, a liar and ..."

"Liar! Liar!" yelled Mika, attacking Marin and knocking him down.

Shana screamed and ran into the yard. A crowd gathered around them. Mika and Marin were scuffling on the ground. Now one and then the other was on top. Their hands were grabbing frantically, legs bending and straightening, teeth grinding, chests heaving and mouths foaming.

Suddenly Marin, very red in the face, found himself underneath Mika. The women shouted and ran away, screaming, "He's going to knife him. He will kill him, he's drawn a knife!"

The word spread with lightning-speed down the street and further, but Marin gathered all his strength, twisting, and with all his might he kicked Mika in the head. Mika dropped his knife. He fell helplessly to the ground and passed out.

Marin got up, shook the soil from himself, found his hat, put it back on his head and, without looking at Mika, he went towards the circle.

Others were pouring cold water on Mika and when they finally managed to bring him round, they wanted to take him home. They took him part of the way, but then he refused their help and sent them back, saying that he did not need them any more, that he would go on by himself. He held his slowly bleeding head, bloodying his hand, as he stared at the ground, thinking. He could see that he had been badly humiliated and he had not expected such a blow. Now the whole village would be laughing at him. They would deride him and he would not be able to hold his head up high any more. He would not be able to look provocatively in the eye of any newly married woman, because he would be ashamed of the poor figure he had cut with Marin today. But no, he was thinking, as he sat down in a doorway, this would not be the end, this would only be the beginning. He would show Marin who he was – how dare he split his head open! He would take his revenge, no matter when, no matter how. He would never forgive him, as long as he lived, no matter what. In this moment, he felt somehow lost, terribly humiliated and offended, and this grieved him frightfully. He did not want to go home and so he walked the streets thinking only about how to take his revenge as soon as possible. And, he thought, he would also show *her* who he was – just wait until she becomes his wife, and then he will show her what he can do and what he is, and she will remember him forever, even when she is six feet under. He decided that Shana would be his wife out of spite to all and that he would do everything possible to make her his wife, and then he would know what to do with her! He would show her who Mika is, the man she has been avoiding and whom she had humiliated.

Chapter 7

Marta angrily slammed the door, causing all the glass panes to shake. She threw a bowlful of potatoes onto the table with so much force that the potatoes scattered all over the floor.

Thrusting her chest out, her hands akimbo, she yelled:

"And I have lived to see this, you black sheep of a daughter! Oh! Oh! It would have been better if I had gone blind and deaf, than to have heard this. This will kill me, drive me mad, I shall have to run away into the wide world begging, as if damned, you wretched woman! I suppose this is the thanks I get for giving birth to you, for bringing you up, for raising you? It would have been better had I strangled you at birth like a newborn kitten and today I would have had peace, I would not have known this terrible disgrace, this great ingratitude! And I have lived to see this from you?"

Marta continued to yell and wave her arms over Shana's head.

Shana laid the sock she was knitting on the table and raised her eyes to Marta, pleading:

"For God's sake, leave me alone for once!"

"What do you mean, I should leave you alone, young woman, when you are bringing disgrace on our decent home?"

"What disgrace?"

"How dare you ask! You still do not get it, you who at the dance have behaved disgracefully with that beggar, as if he were the young man for you. What's more, you shameless hussy, you encouraged him, incited him to attack that decent young man whom you certainly do not deserve!"

"I did not incite anybody."

"Oh no, you did not, but the whole village has been talking about it. There are still people who can see and hear well."

"But Mother, God forbid, since everything has been fabricated by those malicious tongues, there is not a grain of truth in it. If I incited anybody, may God be my judge; but I know my conscience is clear and that I have been slandered."

"And you think you have been slandered: is it not enough that you keep running away from his side in the circle-dance? That you refuse to dance beside him? Is this not enough?"

"But why must I dance beside him? Do I have to do everything he wants?"

"Yes, you do not want to, I know why you do not want to!"

"Why?"

"Because you want to spite me; but just think and remember that you will spite only yourself."

"But why should I want to spite you?"

"I ask myself that! I would dearly like to know that. What have I done to you that you stopped obeying me, that you defy me in everything? You are not defying me when I ask you to respect yourself and to go out with Mika, and in your spite you refuse, you refuse? Is this not to spite me? Well, what is it then? Tell me, what is it?"

"I have already told you hundreds of times not to speak to me about him, I do not want to hear about him, please leave me in peace and stop this acrimonious tirade and nagging to marry him. I cannot bear to look at him, let alone accept his hand in marriage with a joyful heart."

"Oh yes, you cannot bear to look at him, but you can stand Marin, your dear, sweet Marin! Well, well, well."

"Yes, I can bear him!"

"You can, because you do not know what you are doing, because he has turned your head and you are no longer thinking straight. You no longer know what you are doing."

"Have no fear, I know very well what I am doing."

"If you knew, this would not happen. You would understand that he did not care much about you ..."

"What does he care about?"

"What does he care about? I would like to see whether he would be running circles around you, whether he would love you if you were poor, if you had nothing in the world, my sweet child. Do you, stupid girl, really think that he loves you, that he even cares for that sort of foolishness? That is the last thought that occurs to him! He doesn't care. He knows you come from a well-to-do house, and he, the poor man, got greedy for your dowry. That is what he loves, that is in his heart and not you. I am telling you, he would not have taken a second look at you if you had been a poor girl. But he knows what he is doing, he is not mad, even if you are! If you are mad, you cannot see."

"Not true, not true," Shana said, clasping her head, as her eyes began to fill with tears and her chest tightened, as if she could not breathe.

Marta dropped her arms and sat beside Shana.

"Do you think," she started more quietly and calmly, "that anyone else except your own mother, your own parents, could wish you well? Is there anyone else who could love her child more than a mother? Oh, my Lord, how I suffered, how many sleepless nights, caring for you, until you grew up! Nothing was difficult for me, I did it gladly and patiently, because I loved you, because you are my child, because I hoped that you would be sensible and good to me in return, that you would respect me and be obedient, as every honest person would respect his parents! Yes, do not think that anyone else could love you better than I or that anyone else could care better for you and wish you more happiness. I am not a child, my dear, I know what life is about, hence I can speak to you sensibly. You do not know how hard life is today, what times we are going through; therefore, you cannot understand me. Wherever you look today, my dear, everybody looks to his advancement to amass as much as possible, he does not pay attention to those worse off. Everybody thinks of himself and of his own future and nobody wishes himself unhappy, when he knows that he can be happy. If you were sensible you would think about it and you would come to the conclusion that what I have been telling you is the truth, and you would be grateful to me."

Shana stood up:

"I beg you for God's sake to leave me in peace! I would even prefer not to get married at all than to marry Mika. I tell you I cannot do this, do not force me!"

Marta jumped up and punched the table with her fist:

"If you refuse to listen, then get out of my sight! And never again tell anybody that you are my daughter! Go, you miserable wretch, and never dare to appear before my eyes. Shame on you!"

Shana looked at her blankly. She went white and trembled and she almost fell to the floor. She said nothing and went into her bedroom and sat on her bed. She heard Marta's terrible cursing and swearing, and she heard the sounds of breaking bowls and plates. Suddenly she thought about her father's return and what his reaction would be when he saw all this mess. She felt exhausted, lost. As she started to calm down, she began to realise the seriousness of the situation she found herself in. What Marta had just said to her had torn her heart apart, and all of a sudden she became afraid of something unknown, something that awaited her with certainty and something she was moving inexorably towards. She began to think about why her mother would prefer not to see her at all, ordering her to leave home and forbidding her to say to anyone that she was her daughter. And all because she did not want to marry Mika. Who was this Mika and what sort of a man is he? And why should she marry him?

Why him, in particular? Who and what is he? Because he is rich? And only because he is rich? She kept thinking that nobody has asked whether I feel content, whether I like him and whether I will be happy and content with him. All this, because they can see nothing but his wealth, and for this reason only they would hand me to him as if I were not a human being who could think and feel. They would sell me like they sell their cattle: whoever offers more, whoever gives more!

She threw herself onto her pillow and sobbed her heart out. She was filled with a sense of turbulence and her whole life had become obscene. She certainly did not wish to see her mother. An inner voice was telling her: this is not your mother, because a real mother could not sell her child, there are no riches in this world that she could sell her for. Another voice was telling her: she is in error, she does not know what she is doing and you must not hate her; she is your mother. You must forgive her, she does not know what she is doing; lust for the land has blinded her eyes, and she can see neither your soul nor your heart.

Having shed all her tears, she straightened up and placed her hands on her lap, feeling like a shipwrecked sailor who has survived, but sees no help from anywhere, no foothold for a future life, and just moves aimlessly on. Despite these feelings, she still had a goal: she felt strongly about what she wanted. And maybe that was the reason why they forbade her to go out with Marin, maybe that was the reason why she had such a longing for him. Her feelings were stronger than her reason. First love is not calculating, only recognising the beloved. It blazes forth in purity without material interests, and this is why it is so strong and guileless. This was the reason why Shana found it so difficult, because she felt that her love already had such deep roots that the whole of her being would have to be changed if they tried to uproot this love. She could not be without it any more. She felt so alone and misunderstood, she felt that they did not care about her inner life and about the irretrievable value of such a life.

The door opened. Marta's head appeared: "Are you there, Shana?"

"I am here."

"What are you doing?"

"Nothing."

"Stop snivelling and come into the room, Godmother Manda has arrived. Be sensible and do not talk rubbish."

"All right, I am coming."

Shana slowly got off her bed, wiped her eyes and went into the yard. She was going into the room when she heard whistling. At the street door she caught sight of Marko's head. He was signalling with his finger that he wanted to say something to her. She turned round and quickly approached the door to the street.

"Be at the end of the house tonight at 9 o'clock. He will come. Be ready. Goodbye."

"Goodbye."

Marta appeared at the front door: "Who was that?"

"Marko."

"What did he want?"

"Nothing. He asked where Father was."

In the room she was greeted by the sweet and honeyed words of Godmother Manda, who stroked her hair and her cheeks and brought a few apples for her. She spoke about not having visited her for a long time, but that it was not her fault as she had been very busy. Work everywhere to be done, her hands full, not knowing where to start first. Anyway, she couldn't do everything.

Then she asked Shana:

"And where have you been, girl, that you haven't been to see me? I have been expecting you every day, but not a peep out of you. I was beginning to think that you were cross with me."

"You know yourself how it is, she is busy all the time in the house. And anyway, during the week she cannot leave the house."

"Well, you could have visited me on Sunday, at least. For I can see that you look thin and pale and weighed under. You're not ill, are you??"

"I am not."

"You must look after yourself. Your health is most important. When I was young, I was not so sensible either, I did not look after myself and now in my old age I am paying for it. Something always ails me. It is either my head or the small of my back, God alone knows, things come upon me. I have been to the doctor but I feel neither better nor worse. Doctors take your money without making you feel any better. Anyway you must have heard by now?"

"Heard what?" asked Marta immediately, being nosy.

"About Janja Stankich getting married."

"Who is she marrying?"

"Well, Barisha Dekich, that's who."

"You don't say?" said Marta, surprised. "Oh, look at that girl, but is she not marrying Matija Marin?"

"She does not want to. And why should she if she can get a better young man?"

"But she went out with him."

"Indeed, she did, but when she saw a better catch ..."

"And why is Barisha a better catch than Matija?" asked Shana.

"Why?" Marta looked in askance at her.

"Yes, why? What sort of a young man is he?"

"He has five acres of land and a small house, and when his grandmother dies, he will have several acres more. And what has

Matija got? Two acres and a bit of vineyard. And who knows when that vineyard will be his. Because that mother of his is not going to die soon."

"But Matija is a handsome young man, handsome as a young woman, and he is clever, and one does not know what to think of Barisha. He is short, hunched, tongue-tied; he is not fit for the company of reasonable folk!"

"Who bothers nowadays about whether he is handsome or not? It is important that he owns something, that is important, and what he looks like is totally irrelevant. In time she will get used to him and he will be handsome and dear and good. One can get used to anything, especially a Christian soul. Do not imagine that Janja is stupid; she knows what she is doing. She knows very well!"

"And which girl looks for beauty today?" interrupted Godmother Manda.

She continued:

"As long as he is rich, as long as his house is full of good things, that is what matters. And if she wanted love, well, she could have that too: she can find herself anyone she wants, if she is clever. That's how it is, my dear."

"That is not honest at all," Shana blazed, "because when a young woman gets married she should not deceive the one she marries; if she marries him, she should love him. Yes! She should not act promiscuously with other women's husbands or young men, because this is dishonest and obscene!"

"And do you think that he will not deceive her? Do you think that men are saints and that everything they promise will be true?"

"That's even worse, Godmother! It would be better if she did not marry at all."

"Not marry? Remain a spinster? What would she achieve then?"

"She does not have to be a spinster. Why should she be a spinster when Matija would like to marry her, since he loves her and she loves him?"

"He loves her, indeed! I would like to see him find one who is better off and then you would see how much he loved her! This loving thing is nothing. Today here, tomorrow gone! Those who love each other quarrel and fight all the sooner. He would love her as he would love any other."

"If he were honest he would not cheat on her!"

"All young men are deceitful, one and all. Only you girls are stupid enough to believe them immediately when they tell you they love you."

"Well, I know it myself. I have my own experiences so I can tell you. I was young and I fell in love, indeed I did. But when it came to marriage then I looked to marry someone who owned more, who was better. He entreated me so much, he is still alive, this Filip Jozich, saying that he loved me so much that he could not live without me, that he was going to kill himself if I did not marry him. I do not remember any more what else he told me. And on St Michael's day at the parish fete, he bought me so many presents that I could not count them any more. In the circle-dance he was always beside me. But when I got married, he had no intention of killing himself. Instead he too got married, there, his children are all grown up now, some have already served in the army. Don't think that I willingly married my late husband, but eventually I learnt, I got used to him and I became content and I was all right. What's more, I found myself thanking God for such happiness; and anyway God alone knows how it would have been with Filip. This husband of mine died three years ago and I have been left a widow and I can please myself, because I can afford to, I have been provided for. That's how it is, my dear. Every sensible person goes for the mate who owns something, and all the rest is secondary. Love lasts only as long as you are young and crazy, but the riches are always welcome, in old age too. Nobody can live on love, my child, and never will. You could indulge your heart if it weren't for the stomach, one needs to eat, one needs to live. That's how it is, one has to think about that. You have to get married when a good opportunity arrives, because once it is too late, many a girl has regretted allowing a good opportunity to slip by. So my child, you too have to be sensible and respect yourself and your reputation, and people like Marin you simply must ignore."

Shana gave a start at these last words. They felt like a knife piercing her heart. Her eyes flashed, because she now understood the reason for her godmother's visit. She suppressed the fury that suddenly enveloped her and, carefully glancing at Godmother Manda, she spoke:

"You are all telling me to give up Marin ..."

"And that is what you have to do. You have to listen to us because we are older and more experienced; therefore, we know better which young man is more suitable for you, and which is not."

"All right, Godmother, I know you all wish me well and that you care for me. But tell me honestly, from the heart: have you ever heard that Marin is no good, that he is dishonest?"

"I have not heard anything."

"Has Marin been visiting other men's wives, widows and other kinds of flirts?"

"I do not know. I have not heard anything."

"And has Mika done these things?"

"Oh, that is nothing. He is a young man, and young men go to all sorts of places. What can you do, he is young!"

"Oh, really? Has anybody seen Marin going on a binge, accompanying musicians through the village, throwing his money around, falling asleep in the mud until somebody drags him home? And that at home when he wakes up, beating up his mother so that the poor woman has to run to the neighbours, not daring to return home for two or three days?"

"Somebody has filled your head with stories. It is not all true what people gossip about."

"Once I saw her with my own eyes running away!"

"She must have deserved it!"

"Godmother, and what makes you think she deserved it? It is no good defending a bad person, it is no good. You think Mika is better than Marin only because he is rich, but you pay no attention to his dishonesty or whether I would be happy with such a rogue! None of you want to think about that, it does not interest you. You would not have to live with him but I would. My life would be heart-breaking and full of suffering; what good would all his wealth be to me then? What use? Wealth or no wealth, I cannot love him, he disgusts me – so he can go and find a girl to his own taste. I give up the honour of such happiness that I might find in his home; but why do you, who insist that you care for me and for my happiness, then push me into his filth because of his land? Why do you not ask whether I would be happy and content? And would you bear the responsibility for my unhappiness if he started beating me and throwing me out of the house when returning home drunk at night? Where would I go then and what would I do then? What use would it be to me being married to wealthy Mika? Yes! For you Marin is not good, Marin is not to your liking, although he is pure and honest as the day is long. You lust for land, land, wealth! Go then and marry Mika yourself and I wish you luck!"

Shana then turned round and slammed the door behind her so it shook, whilst Godmother Manda and Marta watched in horror.

"Well, well, look at her!" said Godmother Manda in great surprise.

"Well, well ... doesn't she speak like a lawyer! But never mind, let her get it out of her system, we were the same when we were young. She will get over it, she will calm down. That cripple has turned her head so she is now mad. Do not worry about it, I will sort it out, I will help you and it will all end up all right. People's gossip is not always true. From the most insignificant they make a miracle. And if Mika is now leading a loose life visiting various women, he will change when he marries and will no longer care for such things. All young men are like this in their youth until they marry, then they sober up and cleave to their family and take care of the home. He will be the same. Now he behaves in this manner because he has nobody to teach him and care for him."

Marta was wiping her hands on her apron:

"Look, Joza is also greatly interested in marrying Shana off to him. Since he has everything, we too would be better off. I just wish she were a different kind of person, I wish she would try to please him, to flatter him and then happiness would ensue, you could not wish for any better. But she is stubborn and when she gets something into her head, nobody can budge her."

"Try with her in a gentle way. A gentle way goes further."

"I have tried all sorts of things. A nice way and a rough way, and it is all the same. I tried beating her and cursing her and it did not help. I wonder who she takes after in her stubbornness and disobedience."

"Everything will be all right. She is neither the first nor the last who has been disobedient. But you must watch her and not allow the opportunity to slip, because now is the favourable moment and who knows if another one might ever come along. Strike whilst the iron is hot: take the hint and act whilst the young man is willing. I will visit more often to help you."

Godmother Manda got up to go home and at the door she said to Marta:

"I am going now, I have stayed somewhat longer, but you remember what I said to you. Goodbye."

"Goodbye, Godmother Manda!"

Marta turned away, bowed her head and went out to look for Shana.

Chapter 8

In front of his house Marin was checking the grapevine that climbed up to the roof. He had brought with him several canes to prop it up in order to make it grow more tidily and along the roof. He had already spent the whole morning doing this. When the vine was in full leaf and the grapes began to redden and ripen, a pleasant and beautiful shade was to be found in front of the house where he would often spend many hours sitting down with his mother, and where at midday they would eat and talk about many different things.

Marin never neglected this vine, he took great care of it, as something very close to his heart, something he especially loved. He knew that his mother loved this vine, that it had a particular place in her heart too and therefore he wanted to look after it, to keep it in good order. Whilst he had thus been occupied, the sun burned hot from above and the air was so warm that it caused his brow to drip with sweat. He raised his hand and wiped his forehead, then drove the cane into the earth and, looking at the result, he became lost in thought. Only when Marko tapped his shoulder lightly, laughing, did Marin smile and look up at his friend with joy, as if he was extraordinarily happy to see him in his yard.

"You are tidying ... tidying?" Marko remarked, looking at Marin's work.

Wiping his hands on his old and shabby baggy-bottomed calf-hugging trousers, Marin brought a little chair and placed it in the shade of the mulberry tree, whilst he himself sat on a tree stump that lay under the tree, which he would use to chop firewood on.

"I am tidying a bit. It needs doing."

"Yes, indeed …"

"I do not know when I would do it, if not today. I seized the opportunity, a bit of free time, so I said to myself, it will be one thing less to do because who knows when I will have free time again. Anyway I could not neglect the vine. And how are you? What are you doing?"

Marin directed the questions at Marko and, taking out a box of tobacco, rolled a cigarette and offered it to him.

"Well, how am I? So, so. I am getting ready to start the harvest. I have been to the fields and I can see that the wheat is ripe. Thank God, it is good, this year we will not need to complain. It melts your heart just looking at the ears of wheat that are so plump, ripe, and bending with weight."

"Have you come to some agreement about your work yet?" asked Marin, lighting his cigarette and blowing the smoke, looking into the distance.

"I have been to see Stjepan Kolar and he told me to come to work for him. And you?"

"You know where I will be ..."

"With your boss?"

"And where else would I go? I have no complaints about him. He is good to me. He is a good soul. What he has, I get a share of. I feel as if I'm at my own home. Well, I have been with him for several years."

"My boss is rather strange, he would not even give a grain of salt to God. He thinks only of himself, all for himself, as if he were going to live for a hundred years or take his goods to the other world. He is such a greedy man and there is nothing worse than a greedy man. If the truth be told, I do not even like to look at a greedy man."

"Why don't you look for someone else?"

"I would have done it a long time ago but you know how things are, I would not like to cross my sister, because he is a distant relative of her husband and you know that objections would be raised immediately. And then I think, as her husband is all right there, when they can work for him, why not me as well?"

Marko lit his cigarette and returned the box to Marin. He breathed the smoke out, looking at it, and after a small pause slowly said:

"Yes, how are things with Shana? Have you seen her?"

Marin shrugged his shoulders.

"I have not seen her. I do not know what happened. When I sent her the message through you, she did not come, although I waited a long time for her."

"She did not come?" said Marko. "I am surprised. She promised to come. I am sure she was not able to come. Not to worry, you shall see her. I will take a walk there and I will have a word. But it is good that you sorted the head of that one, he will remember you. What a pity I missed that! Had I been there, he would not have got off so lightly. We would have shown him together and he would have remembered forever who he drew his knife at."

"Let him alone! He's no man worth bothering about." Marin waved his hand with contempt whilst looking at Marko.

"He has not yet come across his match, a man who would teach him a lesson. But he might one day. And Joza is just like him. They think if they are rich they can do what they want, to them everything is permissible. You know, I have to tell you the truth. Believe me, I had hoped that Joza would not have turned out to be such a bad man. I knew that he would take advantage of a poor man, I knew that before, but to ruin a man in this way, that beats the lot. This is no man, he has no human soul. My God, we are human after all, and we need to think further than just ourselves."

"What happened?" asked Marin.

"Weren't you in the village on Sunday?"

"No. I was there the Sunday before."

"Oh, yes, I remember, you said you were going to the farmstead. I remember now."

"And what were you going to say?"

"Oh yes, last Sunday a lawyer came to the district and sold the house of Martin Pavich."

"He didn't?"

"As the sun shines," said Marko. "The man owed money to Joza and he could not repay it, and how could he, at this inopportune time? Joza handed him over to the lawyer who in no time at all sold his house. Oh man, I was there, my heart was breaking. When the buyer placed the last fifty dinars and the other man shouted 'third time', Martin went white as this wall and nearly fell down, his eyes filling with tears. He was left totally destitute and he has small children."

"Where is he now?"

"He moved to Marica Tubich, he rented a room and somehow they settled in. You know if I had been in his place I would have broken the snouts of this lawyer and Joza, so they would have been in no doubt whose poor man's property they had sold. Can you imagine, selling a roof over somebody's head? Only a heathen could do that, not a Christian soul."

"He could have waited."

"Of course he could have waited!"

"The man would return the money once saved, and certainly it would not be lost."

"Of course not lost. I know, I was so surprised, there was no word of protest. When his neighbour Matija said 'They sold your house for a pittance', he just went pale and waved his hand. 'He can have it, it will not make him rich!'"

Marin bowed his head and started drawing with a reed in the sand in front of him. He was lost in thought. He suddenly felt a heavy weight on his heart. It was not a great surprise, this news he had just heard from Marko, but even so it filled him with a new wave of bitterness which was spreading inside him more and more. He began thinking about why he was not worthy enough to marry Shana and what it was that divided them. What was it that divided them and what was it that bound them together? These thoughts took root in him and would not leave – they troubled him, troubled him fiercely, made him want to stomp on the ground, push back his hat and run through the gardens, over there through the reeds towards the dyke, and hurtle headlong, until these thoughts were left behind and he had escaped them. If something was separating them, and he could see what that something was, he could also see that something was binding them just as powerfully and firmly, and to find himself between this separation and this binding together was for him dreadful and truly terrible. This was tearing his soul apart: now holding him in hope, carrying him to a higher place, and then again, darkening, everything being destroyed, leaving him in a state of uncertainty which, day after day, was torturing and killing him. Even if he was a poor man, even if he was a servant, even so he would be an honest man, and would have no need to feel shame before anybody, he could look everybody straight in the eye. He never thought that he would find himself in such a situation. Love did not question the possibility of future obstacles, it bound them together, carefree, young, not subject to manipulation, and which now reigned in their souls. That which did not question whether the dream woven with this emotion could ever be realised, whether there might be any differences between them that would divide them or perhaps even separate them one day.

Sitting now, in front of the house and drawing with a reed in the sand, with his friend Marko smoking whilst sitting before him on a little stool underneath the mulberry tree, Marin remembered the first days of his love for Shana, and it seemed to him that he was returning to a beautiful dream when he was so happy, but for such a short time, such a short time. Their love, pure and untouched by calculations and speculations, was born in a field, where everything lives in freedom, in honesty, where nature offers all the beauty of grace to her children, all the beauty of spring! Where bees fly from flower to flower, where birds sing about the throb of nature that God endowed with the life and power of continuous regeneration! He remembered walking from the farmstead to the village and how carefree he felt, how joyful. He did not know about sorrow then, about the pain that hollowed the cheeks and led to a troubled life of true expectations and hopes, but neither had he known about the beauty of love and about the joys it could offer.

And whilst over the village the day had been descending into its first soft and moist shadows of a fresh and pleasant evening and the hawthorn near the path was exuding its scent, with the reeds gently swaying in the light breeze and the cows' mooing heard from afar, he had been walking along the path with his bag casually thrown over his shoulder, whistling a joyful little ditty. Before him, the white village cottages were just discernible, the trees with large treetops and the church steeple that rose proudly above everything. Near the village, Shana was coming towards him. She was bare-headed, her hair carefully combed, smiling. Changeable shadows flitted across her eyes, playing on her white sleeves rolled up to her elbows. In her arms she carried a bowl covered with a kerchief. She looked at him, smiled and walked on, and he turned around and watched her for a long time. From that evening she was constantly in his thoughts, whatever he was doing he was thinking of her; wherever he was, she was beside him in his thoughts. When he was beside her in the circle-dance and when he told her confidentially that he could not bear to be without her, that he loved her, she got cross and left him, running away laughing towards her friends; and when the next day she greeted him, then he felt the power of life, the power of youth. Then the meetings with her ...

Marin dropped the reed from his hand and got up from the stump. He sighed and ruffled his thick black hair. His mother appeared at the door of the house with a rosary in her hand. She shaded her eyes with her hand, looking round the yard, and walked towards Marin.

Marko shook himself. Throwing away the finished cigarette and pushing his hands in his pockets, he said:

"It will be midday now ... I am going, my lunch will be ready when I get home!"

Marin saw him off. Then he paused by the door of the house and, looking back at his mother, he asked:

"Shall we have our lunch now?"

His mother turned round, saying:

"Yes, I was just going to call you."

Marin was pensive during lunch. He was silent, as if lost. His mother noticed that he was again preoccupied with the thoughts that troubled him. She wanted to help him to be happy, to be cheerful as he used to be when he went round the yard singing and feeling carefree and joking with everybody. She wanted to help him recover his previous peace and light-heartedness, because when she watched him like this, a certain disquiet and fear entered her caring motherly heart and a sense of foreboding filled her thoughts. And since she had no peace, even at night, worry enveloped her and she was wondering how best to solve the whole thing. She knew very well that Joza would not give Shana; she had no doubt about it at all, and therefore she continued to be surprised how Marin could even permit himself to fall in love with Shana in the first place, when he could have foreseen that nothing would come of it. Thus, she thought, it would be most sensible if he gave up Shana, let them keep Shana and all their wealth, only let that there be peace and happiness in the house as it had been until now. Marin would easily find a girl of his own state who would not bring sin and quarrelling into their house.

As a result, casting a glance at Marin, she asked:

"What has Marko been telling you again?"

Marin put his spoon down:

"Nothing in particular."

"What did he say, whose house was sold?"

"The house of Martin Pavich."

She crossed herself at these words, looking at Marin in great surprise:

"Only trouble comes from that house. What do you think ... he sold a man's house over his head!"

"What else could he have expected? That one would sell anything in order to amass money, to amass more!"

"He has been like that since I remember him. He is not like other people. One does not see him go to church to pray to God, but his place in the pub is never empty on Sundays. He never buys a drink for anyone and nobody has ever said that he has had a good meal or a drink in his house. And that Marta of his!"

Marin's old mother, waving her hand at her last words and filling their glasses with water, continued:

"It is best not to have anything to do with them. Let them keep their wealth, so far we have not suffered hunger or thirst and God willing we shall not in the future, either. And when you want to get married, you will find yourself a suitable girl and they can keep their Shana."

Marin looked at his mother: "Don't you worry about that so much."

"And who should, if I did not?"

"I will sort it out, leave it to me!"

"But I would suggest that you leave them well alone, because look what happened with Mika. They will think in the village that you covet their wealth."

"They can think what they like, I know that I do not want their wealth. But they cannot order me to either love or not love Shana. If her parents are like that, she is not."

"Well, to tell you the truth, I do not know what she is like, but since they raised hue and cry against you and they want to marry her to Mika, it would be best to let it go immediately and let it all end here and now."

"So Mika can have her, but I cannot?"

"Oh, my son, he is rich and they will give her to him, for you are poor."

Marin scowled and his dark eyes flashed furiously.

"So, just because I am poor, they will not give her to me? And this is the only reason! But they will give her to him because he is rich! Am I not just as much a man as he is? Has anybody been able to find fault with me?"

"No, my child, they have not."

"She can be his because he can buy her, because he has money and land? But she cannot be mine because I cannot buy her?"

Marin got up and started pacing the room uneasily. His face darkened, his mouth shut tightly, and his eyes became bloodshot.

"This means, I could love her as much as I liked, be open with her as much as I liked. She could respond likewise towards me, but none of it would count! He can come and trample on all of this, trample, he has money!"

Marin continued to pace the room, as his mother watched him fearfully and said:

"Well? What can you do when things are as they are?"

"As they are!"

"It has always been like that, a rich man married a rich woman and nobody paid any attention to love."

"That is how cattle copulate. And is this honest, is this human? Oh, they are obscene and disgusting with their heathen calculations. Villains, not people!"

His old mother tried timidly to calm him down, so she waited until his rage subsided a little. Then she got up and opened her arms, as if seeking help from *him* to give her some advice:

"I know you are sensible and I trust you to do nothing that could harm us. Oh, my treasure, do not cause me to have these worries in my old age, to have fears now when I am old. Ever since I learnt about all this, I have had no peace. I live in fear, I am afraid of something bad happening to you, because you know that nowadays there are all sorts of folks around who fear neither God nor honest people. I can no longer go to church ..."

"And why can't you?" Marin stopped and paused in front of her.

"I am afraid."

"What reason do you have to be afraid?"

"How could I not be afraid when Marta sent a message that she would shame me before the whole world, that she would –"

"Who told you that?" Marin blazed.

"Marica Ilich told me that. But I keep thinking: what has she to do with me and why should she shame me before all the world? I did nothing to her. With all due respect, we do not need anything of hers, were it even pure gold! She can leave me alone."

"She has nothing to do with you! If she dared to say anything to you, I would show her! Does she think she can rebuke and shame you, because she hates and curses me? She must watch out, should she touch you or say something to you. I will show them all. I will show all these hypocrites and traders that although I am a poor man and working for others, I can love Shana and that she will be mine and mine alone, and only if she desires that, if she loves me still and if she can endure this hell to the end! I will show them that they will not have it all their own way and that I am not a villain like them in spite of being a 'beggar', as they always call me. This beggar will show them what he can do! Anyway, I have had enough of their meddling and insults, and when my blood boils over, let them watch out! If I am a beggar, I am a man and I am not worse than any of them!"

Marin's face became all red. His lips were quivering, his fists clenching, agitatedly contracting as if he were going to crush everything within reach of his hands.

His hair fell dishevelled on his forehead, his eyes became troubled, darkened and blazing with unaccustomed hatred, so that his mother became frightened and, covering her face with her hands, started to cry. In all her life she had never seen him like this. She never even thought that a man like this could exist in her son. She was appalled at such determination and self-confidence.

He turned round, slammed the door behind him angrily, stepped out into the yard and went into the garden. The rage that gripped him did not abate immediately. His heart was like a cauldron when the liquid in it reaches boiling-point. He paced the garden, but he did not see or hear anything around him. Darkness and hatred veiled his eyes and everything went black before him. Thus, he paced backwards and forwards for a long time, until finally he dropped onto a bench beneath the morello cherry tree, propped his chin with his hand, and found that he was calming down. The garden around him was all green, the full shade spreading above him, and the pleasant scent of flowers and grass soothed his chest, whilst bees were flying from flower to flower. He looked before him and felt life pulsing all around. He saw nature sporting its broad meadows below the garden. A light breeze touched and cooled his forehead. He felt an easing in his soul, the clouds lifting. That dark cloud which covered his eyes began gradually to lift also, and the beauty of nature revealed itself again with its pure, pristine life. When everything had calmed down inside him, when he felt the restoration of his inner balance, he felt sorry for his behaviour in front of his mother. He felt ashamed for his actions, regretting his inability to control himself in order to think calmly and solve the situation.

He got up and went in to see his mother. At the garden gate he found Stanko Zhivich, a friend from his army days, who had worked in the next village as a smithy for some time, but had now moved to town to find a job there. He tried to persuade Marin to come to town with him, for them both to find a job there. He had connections in town, he said, so it would be easier to find a job.

Marin listened to him carefully, but finally declined as he did not know any trade and did not think he would fare well in town. Town was not for him, as he was used to working on the land, he was used to living an ordinary life in the village, and thus he could not live in town. He grew up on this land and if he left it he would lose touch with the land, and would be unhappy. Besides, there was his mother, she could not live alone, it would be too difficult for her.

Towards the evening when his friend left, Marin went to the farmstead. The grain stalks were swaying in the wind before him and around him and it felt to him as if something warm and precious was whispering to him, as precious as a mother's words, as warm as the caresses of the beloved one. For a long time he looked at the large sea of wheat which was being gently engulfed by the night and he felt that a mysterious voice was passing through this enormous plain and that this voice carried within it life and infinite love for the land, and for the infinite trust of those who drenched this plain with their sweat. He listened to the voice of the wheat at dusk, to the mooing of a cow and the growling of a dog, and now it all felt so dear, so close to his heart. He understood the sound of the wheat, the mooing of the cow and the growling of the dog, he understood all of this life where he himself had grown up. He knew that this wheat was not his, that these vast and rich fields were not his, that they belonged to the other, but he felt that they were a part of his life, that he lived with them too, and that he loved them as himself, as his own life, and consequently he could not leave this land to live in the town.

Chapter 9

Since the day of Mika and Marin's fight, Joza had been even angrier with Marin and, to show that he was the boss in his house and nobody else and that every command of his had to be obeyed, he forbade Shana to dance beside Marin in the circle-dance or even to talk to him. And should she disobey his command, then he would show her whom she was disobeying, and who was boss in the house.

Since that day he had also been somewhat afraid that Mika perhaps would not want to ask for Shana's hand in marriage and would prefer to go to the next village to marry someone there. In order to secure Mika for Shana, he sought an opportunity to find him alone so he could chat, but for a long time he was out of luck because Mika had no longer been coming into the village, as before. He also stopped visiting Joza's house. This change of his they interpreted in various ways, but in the end they agreed that everything would have been all right and fine, and they would not have worried and feared so much, had it not been for Marin. He spoiled everything and caused them all this worry. Joza was particularly furious with Marin for even daring to think of Shana, because he saw it as an act of humiliation, seeing him as a fool. How could a poor man, somebody else's servant, someone who was barely surviving, who was fit to look after his pigs ... how could a man dare to even think of marrying Shana? Joza could not get his head round this. This he could not comprehend.

"How presumptuous is all this!" he said repeatedly to Marta, banging the table with his fist.

Marta indeed agreed with him and added many of her own remarks, which made Joza even more enraged, even more bitter. And who fared worst in this situation, if not Shana? The sky was falling in on her and Joza blamed her the most, he cursed her the most, but when Shana saw that she would get no understanding from them, she withdrew in on herself and fell silent. She no longer wanted to go to the circle-dance and she remained at home. Often, she would sit at the window and pensively carry on with her work. There was no joy in the house any longer, her laughter had ceased and the house was enveloped in a gloomy silence. Shana obeyed all commands without comment, doing all the jobs well that Marta gave to her. In spite of this, Marta was not satisfied. She understood Shana's change in her own way.

Thus, when she caught Shana sitting at the window looking pensive and sad, her face pale and looking lost, Marta would feel a stab within her, and she would scowl and become angry.

"There now, she is silent, putting on airs and graces, because she wants to take revenge, to provoke me. She cannot do anything else, so she is trying this way. She is silent as the wall, answering only our questions but not another word. This is all spite, a provocation!"

Thus thought Marta to herself.

So at times there would be real mayhem in the house. Shana then wept bitterly, but she did not resist anything. For Marta, this was even more infuriating and made her more and more suspicious, leading her to imaginings.

That is why, one evening when she was alone with Joza, she said to him:

"I am afraid she is up to something."

"And what could she be up to?"

"I do not know, but something is not right."

"Look, she has calmed down. Maybe, after all, she has recovered her common sense. She does not want to carry on like a mad creature all her life. Leave her alone, let her be silent, let her grieve, and when that is over and she rejects her foolishness *and* that beggar, she will be back to her old joyful self. At the moment, she is still putting on airs and graces, she is probably trying to touch our hearts, but once she herself realises that nothing can come of this foolishness, she will give up and do as most sensible people do. Leave her alone."

"You know, I am worried that something is not right here. I keep thinking that she is perhaps under a spell or something. If it were not so, she would not be so infatuated. She was always sensible and careful in how she behaved, she knew what befitted her. But look at her now! I tell you, I think she has been put under a spell! You will see that I am right. That mother of his is a real witch and she is sure to have done something and that is why Shana is as she is now. Can't you see what she is like and the way she looks? She could not have changed otherwise. As she hadn't been before, she wouldn't be now. This is something else, I am telling you, you will see, indeed."

Joza then started swearing and making terrible threats. He said that he was going to beat up that old witch, pull her hair out, just like a drowned chicken, and she would never think of doing anything like this again.

Marta tried to pacify him, saying:

"The best thing would be if we knew how we stood with Mika. The longer we drag our feet, the worse it will get. Well, to tell you the truth, Shana could run away one night and marry Marin, and what could we do then, what would have befallen us?"

Upon hearing these words, Joza was truly flabbergasted and frightened. Only now, before his eyes, was he alerted to the real danger, which had not occurred to him before, never having entered his head. Now he did not doubt at all that this disaster could befall him. Who knew what was hiding in Shana's head? What plans had she been making? Suddenly it became clear to him that the matter could not be delayed at all and that it had to be dealt with as soon as possible. He therefore ordered Marta to keep an eye on Shana, so not a step could be made without her knowledge, and rest he would take care of himself.

From that night on, Joza had no peace. He was afraid and this fear brought to his plans the insecurity and sense of foreboding that something could suddenly happen at any minute. If Shana ran away, he thought, and even if she were brought back by the police the next day, what would he have achieved? Nothing! This would be of no use. Everything would be destroyed. The news would spread in the village that Shana had run away and shame would fall upon his head and everything would be ruined, all in vain. Once, he even said to Shana that he would prefer to see her dead than to see her bring disgrace on him with her stupidity.

He heard that Mika's reapers were coming to reap any day now, as soon as the sun became hot again and dried the cut wheat that had been rained upon over the previous two days. So he himself went to the field to look at the land, to check the ears of grain and all in the hope of meeting with Mika. Joza had a plot of land under wheat, alongside Mika's crops, and they were separated only by a long, narrow strip of land, of which the ends were marked by thick stakes.

He went there in the afternoon when the heat had abated a little, hoping to find Mika there as well. He carried a thick switch and walked slowly, looking at the crops that spread from side to side into the distance. Before him, the vast plain opened up, endless, lying low as if it could not rise with the great weight of the burgeoning grain. Beside the path stood green mulberry trees and a cart passed by, raising dust. Joza picked a stalk of wheat and crushed it in his palm and there lay the large ripe golden grains. He raised his hand, blowing on his palm so that the grains, along with the chaff, dispersed into the air; then he nodded his head contentedly and pondered on what a good harvest it was going to be, and how full his granaries would be. This thought cheered him up and he felt tenderness in his soul. In some places the harvesters were already in progress. With sleeves rolled up and shirts undone exposing their bare chests, sweating and sunburnt, they swung their scythes tirelessly, whilst the ears of wheat meekly bowed their own napes, falling without a sigh, without regret.

It seemed that they could hardly wait to be freed from the weight that was oppressing them, and they fell peacefully under the sharp scythes, to relax, to take a rest. Women with hooks in their hands followed the reapers, collecting the wheat stalks into sheaves, and then the strong hands of the men bound them with thick ropes made of reeds. Their faces were all ruddy, sunburnt, their hands calloused, hard, cracked and red, but they felt no fatigue, and their eyes brimmed with joy and the desire to work. The sun cast long golden rays, a light breeze appearing from somewhere to refresh them a little. Joza, too, felt a new energy, the desire to work, entering his body, wanting to roll up his own sleeves and join the workers.

But as soon as he moved away from them, he immediately forgot about them and he was carried away by his own thoughts. Again, a dark shadow settled over his brow and the ensuing seriousness changed the look on his face. When he finally arrived at his own wheat, he paused a while, raised his head, and wiped his forehead with his hand. He looked around as if trying to recall something.

He was looking intently in case he saw somebody on Mika's land but there was nobody there. He continued to walk on the narrow path, lowering his head to check which ears of wheat had grain and which perhaps were barren. He came across only a few of the latter and he threw them away happily and carried on walking. Getting to the end of his land, as far as it reached, he took a look at the little valley, which had a slight dip in it and then a little rise further on. His face expressed a light shadow of surprise. He looked again more carefully at the approaching figure. As he shaded his eyes with his hands to protect them from the sun, he saw Mika. He was walking slowly along this valley, climbing with his head bowed, and carrying a straw hat in his hand and a light jacket thrown over his shoulder.

When he came to the top, he waved his hat at Joza and shouted: "How are things with you? Have you come to check whether it is time for harvesting?"

Joza dropped his hand and answered: "Thank God, I am well, but it could always be better. I found some barren ears of wheat."

Mika came close by and then stopped.

"I am not sure really, I thought of starting soon, because the rain could start again later. And now we have good and favourable weather."

"I think the same," said Joza, looking at him furtively. "That is why I came to check. Some people are already harvesting. And why not when the time is right? I will have to start as well, there is no point in delaying. I am not sure where to start, here or over there near the dyke. It looks to me that the wheat over there is better. True enough, here the soil is somewhat worse but it is still good enough. There the ears are bigger and yesterday I checked and I noticed that the work could start."

Joza again got hold of stalks of wheat and picked them. He twisted them, and turning them in his hand, he said to Mika:

"And when will you?"

"Tomorrow."

"Already?"

"I thought of starting today, but I decided to postpone it until tomorrow. I have also told the farm labourers. It seems that a thresher will be on my field, so I have heard. I hope so. I would not need to cart the sheaves too far."

Then Mika placed his hat back on again and fell silent, looking at the little valley from whence he had just come. And when Joza turned round and looked in the same direction, there all over it lay the incandescent sheaves of the sunlit ears of wheat; the whole of the little valley glowing in the blood-red conflagration of an evening sun that was slowly setting behind the tall trees in the distance. Both of them watched this magnificent sight, both of them watched; but each was preoccupied with his own thoughts. They were both glad they had met, but neither would start speaking of the matter that interested them most. Each expected the other to approach it, because by this very fact each thought himself at an advantage. Turning round, they went towards the path whilst the racket of an approaching and receding cart was heard. The cart was coming up fast and hurtled past them. They walked slowly in silence. Mika continued to carry the light jacket over his arm, only buttoning up his shirt; Joza followed him with his head bowed. The night was falling behind them.

The sun, as it was consumed in its conflagration, was about to sink behind the trees; the sky around it was red, draped in crimson. A bird flew over the ears of wheat, a swallow chirped in a branch, and above them a stork flew past with its catch in its beak. Over there, towards the village where the wood ended, dusk with its fine and still warm fingers was weaving the scented penumbral web, and it enveloped the tall trees low down at the beginning of the wood, before climbing higher. Soon the wood became darker, as if wrapped in a cloud that had sprung from within itself, filling it completely.

Joza stroked his moustache and coughed in order to break the silence:

"It seems that we shall have a sunny day tomorrow."

Mika, having looked at the sky himself, said:

"Indeed. So it should be."

"You are probably very busy at the moment?"

"Why do you think that?"

"Well, you must be busy since I have not seen you for a while. Before, we used to see each other more often, you used to come to our house, we used to talk to each other like family, but since then I have not seen much of you."

"You know how it is ..."

"I also asked the wife what was the matter with you or whether you had been ill. But she did not know anything and was surprised herself. She was worried in case something happened to you; that you might have fallen ill."

Mika rejoiced at Joza's words, seeing immediately what he was getting at. Therefore, he said:

"I am wondering what to do."

"About what?"

"I must tell you what I mean. I am sorry that the two of us could not have become better friends, but there it is, what can we do? I thought that the two of us could have come to an agreement like two mates, that you would give in and give me those two acres, but you remained unmoved. As far as I am concerned I could not give in any more because I have already given in too much. Why should I give in, when I could get more from the other party, when I could get more out of it?"

He looked at Joza with a sideways glance, to see what impression his words had made on him.

Joza gave a slight start, paused, and with visible interest asked:

"And which party would you be getting a better deal from? Who can give you more than I can? Is it not a lot that I am offering you? I tell you that it is a small fortune! What more do you want?" Joza opened his arms and looked at him with conviction.

"Indeed, you are right, I do not doubt it, but when an opportunity arises where you can get more, then ..."

Joza interrupted him and looked at his face with surprise:

"And where can you get more? Who in the village is better off than me? True, there are some who are richer, indeed, there are, but they do not have a daughter ready for marriage. The rest are real paupers, they are not for you."

"But there is another one in the next village. A week ago they came to visit me and urged me to take the one who has thirty acres of land. And it was good land, not just anything."

"What is the use of that when the land is not here?"

"I do not mind that at all. She will sell there and with the money, buy here. That is easy enough."

"And who is she?"

"I have not seen her."

"Whose is she?"

"Her father went to America where he got –"

"I heard of him. I know him."

"And why should I miss my chance? No sense."

Joza suddenly found himself in an awkward situation. He did not expect that. He should not have been so mean as he had appeared to be. He should have let him have those two acres, he should have definitely done that. Then, he hoped that Mika would give in, and now the whole plan had been upset.

But he was interested whether Mika had struck a bargain, so he asked him, pretending not to be surprised at anything, not to care too much:

"Have you struck a bargain yet? Well?"

Mika removed his light jacket from his arm and put it on.

"Not yet."

"Are you going to?"

"I don't know, I will see. You know I am not in a hurry. There is plenty of time, because it is never wise to hurry into anything. It is best to think about every matter first."

Mika spoke these words unconcernedly, but he wondered to himself how this miser would respond, now that he was in a tight corner.

He knew that he had to use his cunning. He had to present the situation in the light of this rich woman chasing after him and that he cared little for Shana. He would certainly try to get as much as possible for himself. He thought Joza would have to give in because he would not be prepared to allow the opportunity of catching a rich man like himself to slip through his fingers. Mika knew this and he tried to hide his true interest in Shana and her dowry. And he was not mistaken.

Joza immediately thought he was wrong to have allowed Mika to go. Indeed, he should not do it. He should give him some hope, at least. Even so, he secretly thought that he would not really like to go to the next village because he cared for Shana. Oh, Shana is a maiden without rival. She is worth more than all the riches of that one from the next village.

Therefore, hiding his own thoughts, he said:

"Well, since you have decided, that is it ... I will not spoil it for you. I hope you will be happy. I thought perhaps we could have talked some more to come to some agreement about those two acres, which is why I did not want to give Shana to anybody else. You were always my first choice, but last Sunday I met with the police sergeant who is interested in Shana. He told me about his financial situation and he also said that it was time for him to get married. I knew immediately what he had in mind, what was in his head. Indeed he is a gentleman and an authority figure, but I said to him that Shana was already spoken for, because I was thinking of you. I did not know that you had changed your mind. Now I will go back to him and explain the situation. It will be good for Shana, she will not have to work so hard, the sun will not burn her face, nor will her hands be damaged by work, she will be like a lady without worries. And her friends will be gentlefolk. Indeed, I know that he has a great deal of money, you know!"

"And you say he would take Shana?"

"Indeed he would."

"And you are thinking of giving her to him?"

"Now I think that would be the most sensible. Since the two of us could not come to an agreement, then let it be thus. Who knows, perhaps it is fate!"

Mika walked beside Joza.

The darkness already enveloped them. In the distance the horizon was overcast, closing, and it seemed as if smoke was engulfing it with its penumbral grey, spreading wider and wider.

Around them the ripe wheat was quietly humming, as if penetrated by a mysterious whisper of tranquillity after a blazing day which the hot sun had made drunk with exhaustion, and now gladly surrendered to in the warm embrace of the coming night. Cart after cart was passing at more frequent intervals, hurrying back to the village. Some were returning from their work and others bringing in the freshly cut grass.

During all this time, Joza was thinking that it would be better if he told Mika that things could still be straightened out, but he still expected Mika to make the offer first: to relinquish those two acres. But if Mika should decide against this and persist with his demand, in the end Joza would give in. What he said about the sergeant was only to show Mika that Shana could marry a gentleman. At the same time, Mika thought if Joza would not give in, he himself would start the bargaining again and give in as a last resort. For nobody had forced upon him the rich woman from the next village; he had invented the story to put himself in a stronger bargaining position with Joza.

Whilst walking towards the woods in silence, both were preoccupied with the same thoughts. Each in turn decided to give in as a last resort. Mika also wanted this in order to show Marin that he could get Shana only if he wanted, but even more so it was the matter of those twenty-two acres. And Joza again thought if things could not progress any other way, well, let those two acres go, he was not going to be ruined, and he would certainly know how to exact something useful of equivalent value from

Mika at an opportune moment. He could not wait any longer because Shana had been giving him grief with her obstinacy. He was particularly worried about Marta's suspicions that Shana might run away with Marin.

They were still both walking in silence. Before them, a row of tall trees had already come into view; the trees that stood at the entry to the village. The houses could also be seen huddled close to each other as if they were whispering confidentially amongst themselves.

Mika kept thinking and mulling things over. Perhaps Joza had invented this story of the sergeant to frighten him? And if that was the case, then he had nothing to worry about and would not need to give in. He could wait a little longer. Joza thought the same about Mika, thus he began speculating and plotting anew. The same doubt troubled both at the same time, but neither wanted to open up. Each kept it to himself, each wanting to have the upper hand in the matter. But as they were nearing the village and thinking that nothing would be resolved, an insidious fear engulfed them both: the fear of uncertainty. Each wanted an agreement, but neither wanted to give up anything of his own.

Entering the village, they both stopped. Mika had to go to the right and Joza straight on. They had to part. They bowed their heads as if thinking, and fell silent for a moment. Joza then stroked his moustache and looked sideways again at Mika.

He coughed:

"Well, that's how it is."

"Well, yes ..."

"We do not want to spoil it."

"We do not need to."

"It could have been otherwise."

"If we had come to an agreement."

"If you had conceded."

"Or if you had."

"Well, you know, I would have conceded, but you were stuck on those two acres and you would not budge."

"But neither would you."

"Had you conceded, I would have done too."

"Had you conceded, I certainly would have done!"

Joza said, placing his hand on Mika's shoulder:

"All right, you let one acre of land go. I will also let one go. So it will be neither as I want it nor as you want it. Neither of us would be able to say that he was mean, that he was cheated. There, agree to that and we can make a deal."

Joza stared at Mika intensely, not averting his eyes from him.

"Should I let one go?"

"Let it go and I will also let one go."

"Then it would be ..."

"Twenty-three."

Mika stared into the field. "And Shana ...?"

"How do you mean?"

"Will she agree to ...?"

"You have nothing to worry about. Why shouldn't she? I am her father, she obeys me."

"So, do we understand each other?"

"We do."

"Here is my hand, twenty-three acres and Shana!"

"Agreed."

Mika shook the offered right hand.

They both felt relieved. Each felt that there could not have been any other outcome. All fear vanished from their hearts and a new feeling of a certain subconscious joy filled their entire beings. They did not part, because now they simply could not part. They went to the pub in order to celebrate this day, and the job well-done. They agreed that the wedding would be as soon as the work in the fields had been completed.

The very same evening the news broke out in the village that Shana was going to marry Mika: that it had been agreed between Joza and Mika. Word went from mouth to mouth, and the next day there was not a soul who did not know about this news.

Chapter 10

Thus Shana found herself before the final decision to marry Mika. It is easy for anyone to imagine what she must have felt. How indeed, she began to look at life around her and what she could expect of her future! She hoped against all hope that her parents would give in, that they would not force her to marry against her will, but finally she was convinced that they had no intention whatsoever to respect her will. She was particularly hurt by the fact that they completely ignored her feelings, her pleading for understanding, and that they were prepared to destroy her happiness. What's more, she saw clearly that they did not even try to put themselves in her place, that they ignored her explanations and instead arrogantly and without understanding made plans for her future. She felt utterly humiliated and offended. They had no idea that in her eyes they had sullied her young woman's honour and her self-esteem, and that they had undermined the respect and love she had for them. With conduct like this, Joza suddenly lost esteem in her eyes and she could not feel towards him as she had felt before, she no longer saw in him the father that he had been to her until now, she could not feel for him as she had once felt. She had firmly believed that her parents truly loved her, that she was most precious to them, and at no price would they be prepared to throw her in the path of calamity, but now their true characters were suddenly revealed to her; now she saw through that love and that care of theirs.

She, who believed in goodness and justice, thinking that after all they could not decide about her marriage without her, had now lost all trust in them and felt abandoned, misunderstood, and totally alone. Having now found herself in this terrible situation, without trust and without hope of being understood or helped in any way by them, despair began filtering into her soul and darkening her inner self. Wherever she turned, she remained alone, everywhere she saw only interests, everywhere reigned the greed for wealth, for gain, but nobody wanted to look into her soul … Nobody wanted to question whether it was honest and just to trample on the most sincere and upright feelings in her heart for the sake of wealth and money.

Shana noticed a change in her mother's demeanour. Her face showed an inner satisfaction, her eyes expressed special happiness that can only be seen in the face of people who are particularly satisfied with something they managed to pull off. Shana watched her and wondered why she was so pleased and what it was that gave her such joy.

"Is this a parent's love?" she asked herself and, raising her head, she looked out of the window, as if in a dream, as if none of it was real.

Joza, too, was in a particularly good mood. Having come home, he chatted with Marta about all sorts of things, but this chat was different to before. It was more intimate, as if they had both been warmed up by some new light that illuminated the future. Shana watched, wordlessly, from the sidelines, but a thought kept coming into her mind, God only knows from where, a voice that was speaking to her, speaking quietly, confidentially, so faithfully that Shana surrendered to it like to some consolation: a consolation which had only the aim of easing her pain for a moment, and then leaving her again. This consoling thought gave her no expectation of any realisation of her longings, but in spite of that, it kept returning as an unconscious relief, like a rest for the body after hard work.

It spoke to Shana that she should accept the sacrifice; that in spite of everything, she should not despise her parents and that this act would not remain without reward. Perhaps at the last minute they would understand her, perhaps they would see that they were making her unhappy by tearing her away from Marin. No, it was not possible that they would separate her from Marin, because by this very act the whole of her nature would have to change, everything in her would have to shift. Was it her fault that she loved Marin so deeply? Was this love of hers a sin? So that it can and must be denounced? It was as pure as a fresh morning, when the gardens and the lilacs in bloom exuded their scents; it was not calculating and it came straight from her heart, giving important meaning to her life. If they took away her love, she would be left like a dry branch without blossom, like a withered rose without its scent, without its crown of full bloom. But these thoughts could not keep her going for long, they had to leave, they grew weaker, because the reality before her was quite different. Afterwards, it was even harder and more painful for her. And when she remembered that they were separating her from Marin by force, that they hated him, cursed him and blamed him, though he was blameless, then she loved him even more. He was dearer to her because she knew that he too was suffering. The days were very hard for her, and she felt as if a dark fog were settling into her soul to remove even the last hope, the only ray of hope. She would go to her room and throw herself onto her bed in utter despair, weeping, her heart breaking, with no real hope or consolation forthcoming from anywhere. Daytime passed, filled with some sort of hope, but nights were unbearable; like the bad consciences of sinners, they caused her the greatest suffering. And when she remembered that she had always loved her parents, that she had been obedient to them and respected them, and that now they had withdrawn their love from her, her heart broke and, clenching her hands, she wept helplessly for a long time.

She sighed a lot and kept saying to herself:

"How unhappy I am, how unhappy I am! How joyful I would be if I were poor, possessed no land, and then I would be able to love my heart's desire: what my heart wants and seeks. What is the use of all this wealth when it spells only unhappiness for me?"

During those days that were so full of heavy trials, she often picked up her old prayer book, opening it and praying humbly to the Mother of God to heed her ardent, sincere and devout prayer. Since neither her mother nor her father understood her any longer, since they had become strangers to her, who else could understand her if not the Mother of God, who had loved and suffered the most? Particularly at night, when it seemed that her parents would never understand her, when she foresaw that the whole of her life would only be suffering and sacrifice, then she prayed and invoked God's help. She felt that by herself she was too weak to bear all the trials and thus she sought help where anybody who asked for it, could find it. Thus prayer eased her soul, slowly raising a light of hope and strengthening her; she began to feel the power of prayer and the source of this great consolation.

In this way, her days did pass. The sun was high, scorching the fields, houses, vineyards and farmsteads, and everybody was very busy. Her parents' harvest had also started. The workers went to the fields early in the morning and Joza with them, whilst Shana remained at home helping Marta with cooking and then, along with two other women, she would carry the lunch to the field. Her deftness, her willingness to work, and that joy with which she had used to start every task no longer filled her thoughts and her feelings. Everything she had seen around her and the hope with which she had usually viewed life, often making her feel enthusiastic ... she saw all of this in a different light now. No longer did she think with enthusiasm and joy about her future, about the realisation of her hidden hopes, which often pressed upon her in the middle of the night when lying in her bed, her hands under her head, and outside the air smelling so pleasant and intoxicating, the stars twinkling as if calling to oblivion. How wonderful it had all been then, when her heart would beat joyfully and she would sing, feeling happy about something unknown but pleasant! And now? What was there for her now? What was the use of all the wealth, what was the use of all the flattery of the village women about her happiness, when her heart knew no peace and when her soul was full of bitterness?

Shana thought like this often, and knew that those who envied her this happiness did not understand her. Neither did they know what was going on in her soul. They were only able to speak thus because they did not know her true feelings.

Whilst walking along the narrow path to the field where the harvesters were, Shana looked at the vast plain that lay silently before her in its fruitfulness. Her eyes scanned the tall ripe ears of wheat that glistened in the sun and gently swayed in the light breeze. A warm air hovered over the fields, and the stems of the ears of wheat exuded their scent; birds flew freely in the air and the whole of nature breathed with such ordinary and simple life, so sincere and unobtrusive, that Shana sighed involuntarily, wishing to be a bird so that she could fly to where her heart's desire. To fly and to free herself from the sorrow and turbulence that gripped her, so that she could be happy and joyful again.

The path was soft and straight. She smelled the grass. The flowers exposed to the sun lifted their heads, longing for the pleasant and cool evening so they could surrender themselves imperceptibly to slumber.

As Shana walked, a thought came into her head:

"What use is my wealth to me, what do I want this land full of ripe ears of wheat and this scent of the flowers in the valleys, and the songs of the birds on the branches, and the expensive gold ducats and new clothes ... what do I care for all these when my heart remains empty and my longings unfulfilled?"

The sun was shining and the earth smelt strongly of the ripe ears of wheat. The labourers worked tirelessly in the fields from the early morning. The men rolled up their sleeves and held their scythes and swung them through the stalks of wheat that fell, surrendering, as if they'd been just waiting for somebody to free them from the sun that was discharging hot rays onto the earth and onto the tireless harvesters and women gathering the wheat after them. The sweat poured from the reapers' faces, flowing down onto their tanned and hairy chests, but they continued to swing their scythes as if inebriated with their work.

When the bell of the village church rang, echoing over the sea of wheat and the meadows and fields, the labourers wiped the sweat from their eyes with their shirts, raised their eyes and crossed themselves, leaning on the scythes, saying a prayer to God, who bestowed on the earth the power of continuous renewal and birth, and endowed the clouds with beneficial rain and the crops with the mystery of multiplying. Those tanned and sunburnt faces, which usually displayed prankish behaviour and merriment even in these days of effort and work, now assumed seriousness, tranquillity, and humility; and, with warm and confidential thoughts, their souls came close to the One, who dispersed dark clouds over their village, who sent the clement and useful rain during the days of drought. They prayed to the One who upheld their poor thatched little houses, who caused the hot sun to burn the top of the little hill on which stood the three big wooden crosses. Their thoughts were filled with surrender and trust. For who could keep them joyful and in a good mood during these days of exhausting hard work, as their blood almost boiled with their backs bowed and knees bent, knowing that almost everything would be devoured in tax and excise, and that all that would be left of their hard work would be just enough to feed themselves and not starve? And during those days, they were sustained by the thoughts of Him who gave them joy in the vast fields that undulated in the sun as if in a vast sea. They rejoiced in the mystery of the ripening, in the mystery of the unfathomable life and in the smallest blade of grass in the stubble-field. With their own calloused and blistered hands, they scattered the small seeds into the damp and ploughed earth. They were participants from the very moment of inception of the new life that developed in the healthy and fruitful earth.

They knew that they themselves were the mediators of the mystery of new life flowing inside this soil, which spoke with many languages about the mystery that would be revealed to them one day, when they themselves entered it in order to unite completely with it. Their prayers rose from their chests like frankincense, like the mist in the early morning when the sun rises above the woods, spreading smiles and titillation over paths, ditches, valleys, plains and fields.

When the bells fell silent from the small village church nearby, when peace settled widely over the ripe fields heavy with grain, the labourers ended their prayers. They wiped the sweat off their foreheads with their sleeves, looking at each other with understanding, and laid down their scythes. The horses, harnessed to the carts, lazily chewed the mowed grass, already dry since the morning; they swung their tails restlessly, and shook their thick manes like heavy black fans.

Joza shaded his eyes with his palm. Far away, like a distant memory, the little village gleamed white. In the middle stood a spire, and then, a little further away, stood the tall poplars, proud and still. A cart passed by on the road, not racing in a cloud of dust, but going slowly and sedately.

Joza watched anxiously. He thought that Shana and two other women should be coming any minute now. And he was not wrong. Shana, with the women, descended from the road carrying lunch.

"Here they are, here they are!" shouted the voices joyfully when they arrived, as the women put down their pots and pans and wrapped food.

"We thought you might have forgotten!" said Joza.

"We have not forgotten you."

"The important thing," said Joza, "is that you are here and you didn't get lost! And you have not eaten it yourselves."

"No, no," the women defended themselves. "It did you no harm to wait a little. It has only just gone 12 o'clock. You will enjoy it all the more."

They talked in a simple way, just as their lives were simple; their talk flowed discreetly, affectionately, sincerely and confidentially, as if they were one big family, as if they were all brothers and sisters.

They sat down on the ground on mats, said grace, and started eating. Then somebody shouted that he was thirsty and he asked for water, but there was no water. Others joined in asking for water and hoping that somebody would go and get some. Nobody was willing to go. Everybody waited for a volunteer.

Joza looked at their faces, put his spoon down and said:

"I think there is good water in the well at the end of the field, which belongs to Stjepan Zelich."

"Indeed, it is good, of course it is!" one of the reapers piped up. "Yesterday I had my fill of it. I tell you, it is good drinking-water, and cold."

"Since it is so, here is the bucket," said Joza. "Shana could fetch the water!"

Shana was standing on the side.

"I can go," she responded, picking up the bucket.

"But fill the bucket to the brim because we too are thirsty," the women laughed.

"Do not worry, there is enough water even if there is no wine. I will bring all the water your hearts desire. At least that is easy, plenty of water. If only everything else were so easy ..."

Shana took the bucket and went to fetch the water. As she walked on, she looked at the amount of work the harvesters had done and how many sheaves they had tied. But when she moved further, her own thoughts preoccupied her again and she failed to notice how many red poppies were still scattered within the uncut wheat, and how the ears of wheat were bending in the longed-for wind. In the distance, she did not see the gloomy and darkening sky, a sky which was beginning to mourn for someone.

She did not feel the air becoming cooler and more scented; she did not see the swallows flying with wings wide open and quickly disappearing behind the bushes. Before her, she saw a path covered with grass that had not been trodden down, although she could see footprints. Her long and luxuriant hair fell over her shoulders, her bosom was rising and trembling. When she looked up, she saw only an ordinary draw-well in front of her. The draw-well was askew and it was obvious that not much water had been drawn from it. Here, the shepherds would usually come to water their flocks or the horses would be watered here after the ploughing. Around the well grew a fine and shiny grass that had been completely trodden down. Shana dropped the well-bucket into the well, pulled it out, and started pouring the water into her bucket; then she thought she heard a rustling sound behind her. She finished pouring the water into it and turned round. Marin stood before her motionless, and without a word.

They looked at each other. Shana dropped her gaze and trembled. Only her head registered, "It is he, it is he! The one I have not seen for a long time!" Several Sundays had seemed to her an eternity. He stood quietly without a word and did not move. She did not know what to do. He appeared so suddenly when she expected him least, that she felt off-guard. She bent down, wanting to pick up her bucket and go.

"Shana," he said, looking at her intently.

She lowered the bucket.

"Are you leaving already?" he continued.

"I am in a hurry."

"Where to?"

"There!" and she pointed with her hand. "They are thirsty and waiting for me."

"Is not my soul thirsty too and waiting for you? Their thirst will be slaked by the water, but what will slake my thirst if you are gone? Oh, what am I saying? What is coming into my head? Forgive me, Shana, I forgot that I should not speak to you like that. I have made a mistake. Forgive me! I have no right to bother you and to spoil your happiness!"

"What happiness to spoil?"

"You know. I do not need to tell you?"

"I do not understand you."

"What do you not understand? The whole village is talking about it. Every child knows about it – and you do not?"

"What is the whole village talking about?"

"Well, that you refused me, that you never loved me, that you only trifled with me. And that I was blind and I was only greedy for your wealth. That is what is going round the whole village. They also say that you are laughing at me, because I am chasing after you and that I am mad and cannot see it. You know that I never took any notice of the village gossip, but I felt pain when I heard that they accused me of greed for your wealth and that it turned my head. But believe me, so help me God, this God who knows very well that this is a lie, so help me God, I never wanted your wealth."

"I said nothing to anybody."

"To anybody?"

"Not a word."

"They are lying again! All of them!"

"They are lying, Marin."

"And what have I done to them for them to treat me like this? What have I ever done to them? Have I ever said a nasty word to anyone, have I ever done something evil to them? Why are they like this? Instead of repaying love with love, they repay it with hate, and instead of comforting me and showing me compassion, they attack me and rejoice in my adversity. Are these my brothers, who I can trust in this adversity? Are these my brothers? Well, never mind, I thank them for this too. Everybody has a right to humiliate and slander a poor man without being called to account by anybody. Thus, when I felt so alone in my poverty, when I realised that man can have a friend only when he can help the friend, when he is of use to him, when I saw that they did not understand me, then I hoped that there would be one who would think in the same way as I did and felt the same. And it was you. You were that bright light on the horizon of my life, you were my hope and my consolation, you were my life!"

Marin bowed his head. A vast and immense sea of golden wheat glistened in the sun and revealed to him all its riches, its opulence. The tall stalks of the maize stood motionless, as if longing for that dark point on the horizon to spread, to develop into a damp cloud and for the rain to pour down on the leaves and on the corn cobs in full bloom: the cobs that hung helplessly on the stalks.

Marin continued:

"And this bright hope of my life has gone. I can no longer see it. Believe me, I can no longer see it. Everything has gone. And now ... now there is only emptiness in my bosom, endless emptiness. I look around me and I can see this land where I was born and grew up. I can see these paths where I skipped, strong and happy, I can see these blessed ears of corn which are God-given, but when I take the spade to dig, the scythe to mow, or start any other task, there is no more joy or will to work in me as before. There is no more joy, because I see no reason for my work. I do not know who I am working for; who I am going to make happy and help; whose life I am going to make sweeter; and who is going to sweeten my life. My heart is empty, there is no longer a bright light there, and I leave the scythe in the grass, the hoe in the soil, and I wander off, aimlessly, just to keep moving, keep going on and on, until I find my lost serenity!"

Shana watched him. Those eyes of his, that once used to look at her with so much warmth and kindness, were now clouded, and their gaze was vague, lost. His face, which used to be as rosy and smooth as a young woman's, lacked all colour now and had lost all its freshness. His cheeks were pale and sunken, his forehead was creased, and around his mouth played a spasm of the hidden grief which lay deep inside him like a huge stone. He was a shadow of the former Marin.

"What have I done wrong?"

"What have you done wrong?" he laughed, lowering his gaze.

"Have I wronged you in some way?"

He did not look at her.

"I am suffering as much as you are. It is no better for me."

He raised his eyes to her and said:

"So why did you willingly agree to marry Mika? Why did you say in front of others that you loved him, that you finally saw the light and that when you were thinking of me and when you were with me, you were crazy?"

His gaze penetrated into her pupils, sinking deeper and deeper.

She laid both hands across her bosom.

"I have said that? I …? Oh! What have I lived to see? How mean and vile are these people! They have no fear of God and of His justice! They are not afraid of the punishment that can strike them at any moment. They disgust me – they are mean and vile in my eyes! Oh! If I could just get away from here, far away, where I could not see their pharisaical gazes, where their heathen and godless words could not reach, to go away to find peace in pure surroundings to think my thoughts and have a rest. I am choking amongst them, my breast is oppressed and I cannot breathe. I said nothing to anybody, I did not promise anything to anybody."

Marin trembled. A flame of light glimmered before his eyes. His arms moved.

"Shana, is this really all a lie? All of it?"

"It is all a lie! A vile, obscene lie!"

"Ah, you can see, I am so tired, my head is so heavy that I began to believe these lies. Forgive me! I beg you. You can see that I feel lost. And then … and then what is the use? You know yourself, your father said, that when the work is over and when autumn comes, there will be the wedding, and Mika will take you to his abode."

"He will not live to see it! He will not, because I do not love him, because I cannot bear the sight of him, because he is unclean and bloody in my eyes. I would prefer to remain a spinster than go to his abode, I would prefer to have my arms chopped off to my elbows than caress him with them, I would prefer to gouge my eyes rather than look on him as my husband! I would find the branch on which they hanged me easier to bear than him."

In the distance, thunder could be heard. Something vague and unclear rumbled and that dark point became bigger. A lark flew over Marin's head. Somewhere a stork clacked in its clear and cracked sound. The air became heavier, and oppression settled over the corn on the cob on the maize stalks. The jangling sound of a scythe could be heard from the end of the field. It was a reaper skilfully sharpening the blade of the scythe with the stone to sharpen it, in order to swing the scythe at the bottom of the stalks, which would then fall in a wave-like motion like silver scattered over stones.

"If they force you to marry Mika, if they ignore you in spite of your opposition?" asked Marin.

"I cannot imagine that. I just cannot get my head round this. It seems to me that it is a nightmare and I cannot wake up."

"I cannot carry on like this," said Marin. "I cannot bear it. I have stopped seeing my friends. I flee away from the village into the fields to find peace and silence, just to avoid people, not to see their faces full of nasty malice and disparagement. Today, also, I walked aimlessly, and by chance came across you. As if God himself led me here with his mysterious and unseen hand. Shana, I am asking you, come with me and we will go away and marry. If you love me, you will leave those who are choking our happiness, those who think only of themselves and of their small interests. As you can see, the land is vast, as vast as infinity itself, and there too, far away, where our eyes cannot reach, there too life is lived, there is our deliverance."

He came closer to her. He took her by the hand:

"I will work again, I will work from early morning when the sun starts rising until late into the night, I will work and work very hard, because I will know that all my efforts are for you, that I will find you at home when I return and that you will understand me, that I will not be alone amongst strangers, as I am alone here amongst those who know me. And I will buy you a necklace as no woman here has, and I will buy you dresses and you will not have to feel ashamed before anyone."

Shana watched him warmly with eyes full of anxiety. A dark shadow fell over the sun and the well, and over both of them and over the whole field. In the distance the rumbling sound was becoming louder and the ears of wheat began trembling restlessly as if in the foreboding of a thunderstorm that was about to pour down onto their heads. And the stalks of the green maize began bending their slender necks.

Marin and Shana faced each other deep in their thoughts, as if they themselves were sprouting from this fertile earth.

Equally, as with this wheat which was ripe for harvesting and was to be made into a delicious home-made bread, so these two had also ripened to life; but they did not know whether the scythe of injustice would cut them down helplessly under its blow, or whether they would enter a new life, to be reborn through their suffering and their misery.

Suddenly a voice was heard:

"Shana, Shan-a-a-a!"

The voice was becoming louder, more astringent. Shana trembled and quickly took her bucket from the ground, grasping her bosom with her left hand.

"It is him … him, my father."

She barely finished the sentence when Joza appeared out of the maize field, sullen and bad-tempered, holding a whip in his right hand.

Marin and Shana looked at each other.

"Ah, here you are, girl!" yelled Joza. "You went to fetch the water and started flirting and disgracing me. What time did you leave to fetch the water? Those people over there could have died of thirst before you decided to bring it to them. What time did you leave? You could have been to the village and back by now to fetch the water, never mind from here. Is that how you obey me? Is that how you respect your father? You miserable wretch, you shameless hussy! You came here to meet with this wastrel, this degenerate of the village, so that others from the neighbouring field can see you and laugh at you and at me!"

His eyes blazed furiously and horribly. That low forehead of his was frowning even more and it darkened threateningly, his lips trembling and his hands moving convulsively as he continued yelling at Shana.

"Get out of my sight! Get out of my sight forever! I would prefer you to drown yourself rather than to disgrace me like this in front of the world."

Whilst Shana went off crestfallen with tears in her eyes, Joza turned towards Marin:

"And you, how dare you attack my daughter, when you know you are worth nothing, not a penny!"

"In your eyes I am not worth anything, because you cannot see that I could be of any use to you. I have not attacked anybody. If I meet with someone, nobody can forbid me to talk with that person sincerely. There is no sin in talking to anybody. And if you thought about it calmly and fairly, you would see that I speak the truth."

"What do I care for your ramblings? I do not wish to listen to you. You cannot lecture me, the first farmer in the village. I am the farmer who has done so much good to others that they should kiss my heels out of sheer gratitude."

"I think you overrate yourself," Marin laughed wryly. "I do not think that it is quite like that."

"What is not quite like that?"

"I do not know what you think, but I consider that it is not a benefit to have the house of a poor man sold over his head, all he had left, and then throw him out onto the street with his small children and his wife."

Joza blazed with anger at these words and started yelling horribly so that his voice echoed over the fields and was lost dully in the distance where the sky was becoming murkier and increasingly threatening.

"You dare attack my honour? You scoundrel, you bastard, you are still wet behind the ears!"

He raised his whip and lashed out at Marin's face. Marin trembled and touched his forehead, snaking across which there was an angry red weal. He clenched his fists and he felt a rise of inner rage and bitterness that had been accumulating from day to day.

And now this humiliated and ridiculed man, who was aware that he too was a man, who had his human dignity, having understood that he must have and find his justice … now, the realisation had awakened and blazed from deep within him for him to seek his justice himself, where his neighbour refused to give it to him. A dark and weighty rage clouded his eyes, the rage that was akin to a deep rumbling thunder, coming closer like the wind that was now bending the ears of wheat to the ground and was shaking the stalks of the maize.

Joza stood before him. He stood there like an embodiment of filth and obscenity, meanness and inhumanity, the man who was the cause of grief to many hearts and who had caused many a mother to shed bitter tears because of his loan-shark activities.

"Get out of my sight and never harass my daughter! She has her young man, who she will marry. You go begging with that old bitch of yours, who never taught you how to respect me!"

Marin glared at him.

"What has my mother ever done to you? Why do you slander her, who raised me and cared for me honourably?"

"Ha, ha, ha! Here, I will repay you for this care of hers!"

Joza swung the whip, but Marin jumped, grabbed his arm, snatched the whip and threw it into the maize field. With his left hand he seized him by the chest so Joza's shirt tore, and with his right hand he grabbed him round the waist so he had difficulty breathing.

Around them the wind was blowing and rumbling, bending the stalks of the wheat and the corn, the lightning striking and the thunder grumbling treacherously; and this hoarse sound of the thunder was shaking and breaking somewhere in the heights as a long suppressed rage, now breaking off its fetters, emerging enormous and powerful to spill out into the flood of release.

"Let me go!" moaned Joza.

"You can see, I should really throttle you like a dog, so you drop dead, so you could never again raise your heathen hand against anyone."

"Help! Help! He will throttle me, help me, folks! Ohhh!" Joza croaked.

His voice was trembling with fear, he was shrieking, the lightning striking, the wind howling, and the rain coming down in buckets. The thunder shook and the lightning struck somewhere, and the loud crash echoed eerily around them. Intermittent and indistinct voices could be heard from somewhere.

"No fear, I will not throttle you, because you do not deserve it. I do not wish to foul my hands. Go, I detest you, you are disgusting with that gross and twisted face of yours. But remember I will not allow you to curse my honest mother, who, albeit poor, is decent and worth more than all the wealth that has blinded you. Go, go!"

Having said that, Marin pushed him away. Then he ran his hand over his forehead, turned, and disappeared into the maize field, whilst thunder and lightning continued, and the sudden heavy rains carried on drenching the earth all around.

Chapter 11

Autumn could be felt in the air and in nature. It came over the fields, bringing the fruits of the earth into the granaries, attics and cellars; it laid waste to the gardens and emptied the birds' nests, leaving a pleasant scent in the harvested vineyards, narrow paths and sombre-looking woods; and it turned the water green in the narrow dykes which meandered below the village. Days turned quieter and became more collected. This was reflected in the faces of the people and in the way the women moved. Sometimes even children would stop suddenly and look thoughtfully into the distance, as if surprised by something.

Autumn walked the streets. It was slowly marching from morning till evening. At night, it would nestle in the foliage of the mulberry trees that stood to attention in the streets in front of the houses. When at dawn it would wake up and move on, the yellow leaves from the trees followed in its wake and it would herald the promise of tranquillity and restfulness. Since the beginning of the rains, the village seemed gloomier, and there was a feeling of suffocation hanging in the air, standing still for a long time in the form of a grey mist. Paths turned muddy, cartwheels sank into mud, and horses pulled with difficulty these carts that were loaded with the yellow, damp, harvested maize. Even the paths and roads, which only a little while ago were firm and dry and safe to walk on without fear of losing one's shoes, breathing potholes had become puddles.

For several days it drizzled steadily and monotonously, causing everything to feel gloomy and meaningless; everyone was aware of feeling oppressed, but was unable to put into words what was troubling them. Even the houses were silent, withdrawn, as if afraid to look out onto the streets, as if tired of the semi-darkness and oppressive shadows that dragged themselves sluggishly and sleepily around the rooms from early morning to late at night.

During one of those rainy days, Shana sat at the window, working at her embroidery. The street was empty as if the whole village was suspended in time, not a living soul in sight. The evening was approaching and spreading its ever darker and thicker web over the yard, over the muddy path, and over the room itself, also filled with darkness. The only thing to be heard was the regular ticking of the weighted clock on the wall. Shana sat near the window in silence. She was alone. Joza and Marta were working at something in the storeroom. Only their unintelligible voices could be heard from time to time, and then everything would go quiet again and the previous feeling of stagnation would return. Shana felt that this semi-darkness would last forever, that it would oppress her bosom forever, and she longed for the sun and for her freedom. She wanted to carry on with her embroidery but could not. Even if she started, her hands would stop by themselves, her gaze involuntarily rising and wandering without expression over the beds and tables and through the murky windows into the street. She could not work; she had no desire. An absent-minded tiredness invaded her limbs so that even her movements became sluggish, without volition and with no élan. Her soul filled with a hidden indifference towards everything around her; and then, in the depths of her soul, the pain appeared, quietly and almost imperceptibly, only to turn into a fear which without warning flowed through her being. It was the fear of the thing that was coming closer every day, the fear she felt in the cold droplets of rain crawling down the misty windows.

She stared fixedly at those droplets and a thought appeared from somewhere deep within her:

"What am I living for at all, what use is my life? Have I not the right to live and have I not the right to run my own life? Why am I in this world and does this have any meaning? Am I here just to work from morning till night, to keep quiet, and to obey others' orders? Have I no right to the joy and life that I feel powerfully within me, and that demands realisation? Is it fair for others to run my life, when I know that I am a human being and that I must have my human rights? Work, obey, suffer, marry the one your parents find for you, and then you are an honourable and good daughter, then you will be praised to the sky; but if I ask to have the demands of my heart to be taken into account, if I say that I cannot accept those orders and their wishes for me, then they will yell at me, revile me and scream at me that I am dishonest, a shameless hussy. The whole village will join in and they will brand me as the personification of depravity, waywardness and spite. And what is this spite? Simply the fact that I cannot agree to marry a man I do not love; that I cannot bear, before myself, my shame at their solution: at the thought of being sold, sold as cows, sheep and goats are sold, as chickens, butter and cheese are sold. And what use is this life if I must forego so much? Why has God given me reason, if I am not allowed to use it?"

For a long time she gazed through the window-pane. For a long time she surrendered to the thoughts that were attacking her with terrible speed, and within her disquiet and dark rage were rising and tearing at their enveloping web.

At that moment the door opened and shut. Somebody said something, but she did not even turn around. She continued to stare through the windows, given to her thoughts. Light steps walked across the room and stopped behind her back. Silence fell.

Two hands touched her shoulders.

"Who is it?" Shana asked, and turned round quickly.

"Do not be afraid. It is me. Have I startled you?" replied Mika.

"You? Hmm!" Shana laughed and drew with her finger on the steamed-up window. But her laugh was dry and bitter.

"I came to visit you. Your parents said you would be here working at your embroidery. I like to come and see you and be with you."

"You may like it, but I do not."

"What have I done to you that you do not like me? Have I done something bad to you?"

"And you dare to ask?"

"I ask you because I think you have treated me unjustly and I do not deserve for you to treat me like this."

"If you have not yet understood that I do not want your company, then you never will. I have had enough of this. There are limits, there are boundaries and when they get ignored, then ..."

"But I never wished you ill, I have always wished you well."

"If you have always wished me well, why don't you leave me alone, instead of following me around and bothering me? Leave me alone and do not ever darken my door, because I have suffered so much on your account. If you had any honesty and human pride, you would leave me alone and give up this nonsense, for nothing will come of it!"

"You need to understand."

"I understand you very well."

"If only you could understand?"

"Then I would allow all of you to do with me as you wish. All of you want that. But when you see that I cannot bear you and that you make my life miserable, why don't you go then and find yourself a wife, who will love you and be your match, and leave *me* alone? In the village there are plenty of those that you may be able to buy easily and do with them whatever you want!"

Mika's face darkened. His lips twitched and a vague smile appeared on them.

Shana looked at him:

"If you had ever wished me well and wanted to be my friend, I beg you to go away from me and never return. You do not know how awful I feel inside! I cannot do what you want! I feel I could never give you what a wife should give her husband! I could never cleave to you with my whole heart and soul, because you would always remind me of my lost youth and of my shattered hopes. I know I am different from other girls, who would jump at the chance to have you. You can see yourself that there is no connection between us; that we do not belong together. Therefore, I beg you to understand that this is the end. Since they cannot take it into their heads, since they cannot grasp that I cannot ignore my feelings just like that, since they cannot understand that I am not interested in your wealth, well, at least you show yourself to be a man and understand this and leave me in peace, and I shall be grateful to you."

Mika stood before her somewhat lost. He never imagined that she would come before him with thoughts like these. Nothing was further from his mind. Now that everything had been revealed before his eyes, he felt helpless before her, for she had spoken openly to his face what she thought. He wanted to say something to her, but his thoughts made no connection. He wanted to appear magnanimous, but he did not know how or what to do. He grasped that she disarmed him and that saying anything would be useless. He felt a burning pain inside him, dull and heavy, and he pressed his lips tight and bowed his head, pawing the ground with his foot. He could not look her straight in the eye. Neither could he leave without a word, without explanation: he just could not. He could not, because if he did, he felt this would be the loss of everything. She appeared to him totally different from what he knew of her and imagined her to be. He saw that she was not like many other maidens in the village, who were not capable of thinking for themselves, and whose greatest interests were how to dress, how to use rouge, how to enjoy good food and how to marry into a rich house. He saw that here was a young maiden who thought for herself, and who respected herself and held to her own opinions. Now she appeared much above him and even more out of his reach. He now realised that he needed a great deal of help to win her over, but it also became immediately clear that he would never be able to do this, because she would stick doggedly to her own ideas. Even so, he secretly plotted revenge, because he fancied that it was only her pride and her stubbornness that had to be crushed, one way or another. No matter what, he had to do it, as he could not give in because the whole village would deride him, laugh at him.

"Right," he started, "since you do not care for me and since you are sending me away, I will leave until you change your mind. I can have even better girls than you, ten on each finger as soon as I wave my hand, but in spite of that, I think it would be wiser if you came to your senses whilst there is still time."

"I am sensible enough."

"I can see. Your head was turned by that –"

"Nobody turned my head. I know exactly what I am doing and nobody needs to teach me."

"You would know what you were doing, if they pulled the reins in a little, thus softening your wilfulness."

Turning towards him and looking him straight in the eye, she said: "Listen. I said my piece and I think you know how things stand now. I do not wish to see you. There has never been anything between us and there never will be. You go your way and I shall go mine, and let us trust in God."

"What if I refuse to go?" he said, smiling wryly.

"Then I will go!" She turned round and slammed the door after her.

Mika was left alone in the room. He stared at the closed door and did not know what to do. He did not expect such treatment from her. He cast a glance around him.

Her embroidery lay on the table at which Shana had sat until his arrival. Rain splashed against the window-panes and the sound of a voice calling could be heard in the street. He could hear the sounds of a cart passing by with difficulty through the mud; a noise in the yard; and a ladder squeaking outside. He again looked around, closed his fists and, his face darkening, said to himself: "Just you wait, I will yet teach you sense, as soon as you cross my threshold. You may be stuck up now and strut, but this too will end, it will not be long!"

He was about to leave but the door opened and Marta entered, rubbing her hands with her apron.

"Are you alone?" she said, wiping the window-pane with her apron and looking out into the street. "Go on, sit down, why are you standing? Joza will be here any minute and we will light a candle. It is getting dark in the room, one can't see. Today we carried the corn to the attic and we have just finished. There is always something to do. Well, and how are you, anything new? How are yours at home?"

"They are fine. As usual. Time goes by. My mother is busy with the house and I have come to see what is happening here in your house and to see if there is any news."

"It is good to see you here. Just to have a little chat. But where is Shana, where has she gone to? I thought she was in the room, but she is not here, I will call her this minute."

She went to the door and shouted:

"Shana-a-a!"

Then total silence.

Joza came in through the partially opened door. He adjusted his old, worn fur cap, approached Mika, kindly shook hands with him, and said:

"How are you?"

"I am well. I am well."

"Well, thank God for that. As long as your health is good, everything else will be good. God willing, we poor things will be well too, but, to tell you the truth, I have not felt really well these last few days. I seem to have caught a chill or something: the small of my back is hurting and I have a cough. What will become of me? Only a few days ago I felt strong and healthy, like a rock, but now my legs are all shaky."

"You will have to take to your bed. There is nothing for it but bed. Otherwise you might get even worse. You should call a doctor too."

"Ah, what doctor?"

"To check you over and find out what is wrong with you. To treat you."

"He will not enter my house. He doesn't know anything. I used to go to him, but he was of no help. The old Janja used to help me with her herbal remedies and her prayers, but he never did. He would come and tap me now here, now there, and it was immediately 30 dinars. He thinks money drops from trees into my lap."

He slowly lowered himself into a chair and started rapping the table with his fingers. It was obvious that he was not well, his face even gloomier now and his eyes darkened. His dark skin had become even darker and fatter, and his moustache hung low as if dragging him down towards the earth.

Silence fell between them.

Darkness slowly enveloped beds, tables, the pictures of the saints on the walls; and from outside, the wind was heard blowing round the house and hastening through the garden towards the meadows and the dyke.

"Where has Marta got to now?"

"Perhaps she was delayed," said Mika quietly.

"She needs to light the candles."

"We can talk in the dark too."

Joza got up. He went to the window looking for the oil-lamp, but it was not at the window. He looked over at the bedside table, but it was not there either.

"Where did she manage to leave it this time? One can never find the things one needs. Things get mixed up and when you want them they are not there, you can kill yourself looking for them."

Marta entered the room.

"For God's sake, where have you been?"

Joza reproached her, rather grumpily.

"We are sitting here in the dark and you are not here."

"I am here and I will light the candle now."

She brought a candle from the kitchen, lit it, and placed it on the table. A pallid yellow light shone on the table and on their faces. It was no longer possible to see outside through the window. The room was filled with a pleasant staleness and a kind of vagueness, and those in the room felt they would like to break the silence with something, but could not find the words, and whatever sprang to mind seemed meaningless. Marta pushed her hands under her apron, uneasily casting glances at Joza as if she were afraid of something, as if something were out of order. It felt as if she wanted to say something, but could not at that moment.

Joza coughed. "Bad weather is on the way. Rain, rain and mist."

"It is the time of the year," added Marta.

"Well, any news in the village?" Joza asked, looking at Mika.

"Hmm, there is this and that."

Marta asked: "Do tell, is it true that Marija Katich is marrying Matija Shimunovich?

"So they say, I heard it myself."

"Well, whatever next?" added Marta, in surprise.

"I would not have her if she were made of gold, never mind the way she is, after the way she behaved. She is a shameless hussy, running around dark allies with everyone that offers. Junior clerks, financiers and even the gendarme of the village, you name them, they had her. To marry one like her is a real disaster for a family."

"Don't his parents know about it?" asked Joza coolly.

"What is the matter with their eyes?" said Marta, nodding her head importantly.

"And his father behaves as if he knew everything," said Joza. "He dabbles in politics too, as if that were any use to him. If he were a good father to his son, he would show him what was good and what was not. The father is the head of the family and he has to be obeyed by all in it. In the family it has to be clear who commands and who obeys."

"Indeed, you are right," Mika agreed and secretly rejoiced. He rejoiced because he hoped that Shana would have to obey her father and marry him, since her father gave his honest word to him. She would be an easy target and, later, he himself would teach her who was the boss that had to be obeyed. Thus he thought the present moment was the right one to mention something about himself and about what they had agreed upon.

With a frown he addressed Joza:

"To tell the truth, it would be good to discuss when we should have the banns in the church for Shana and me."

A total silence fell in the room. Joza did not move. He only touched his moustache with his right hand and raised his head slightly.

"When?" he said, slowly as if thinking about something.

"Yes! I think it is time."

"Well, Marta, what do you think?"

"I think the sooner the better. There is no point in stalling and dragging our feet."

"Well then, when do you think I should contact the parish priest?"

"You can do it tomorrow. It is Tuesday today, isn't it?"

"Yes."

"On Sunday the first banns can be read in the church. The Sunday after, the second, and the following, the third. We could have the wedding in a month's time. I think that would be the most sensible."

Mika said:

"In that time I too could get everything ready for the wedding reception. I would be able to get all the necessary things: there are so many little things that are needed in cases like this, things that have to be ready in advance. There will be a lot of work in the house as well."

Joza added:

"So, as we agreed, so be it. But Marta, where is Shana so late at night? She is usually at home, never going out, and now, when I want her, she is not here."

"She is in her room. I was with her a minute ago."

"What is she doing there?"

"She says she is not feeling very well so she lay down. It is not at all surprising, the weather being so unsettled and damp, it is enough to make you ill. My head too has been aching all afternoon and I feel battered, I can hardly drag myself around the rooms."

Mika stared in front of him and appeared not to hear what Marta was saying, but he did notice that Marta was avoiding his eye, for he knew the real reason for Shana's absence. What's more, Marta knew that he knew, and she was covering everything up with pleasant words in order to smooth the situation. He said nothing in reply.

He got up and straightened his coat, saying:

"Well, it is dark already, I am sure my mother will be waiting for me with my supper."

"You could stay a little longer," suggested Joza.

"Next time I will do. And so, let it be as we agreed."

"Indeed, no doubt about that. I will take care of everything. Or will you go yourself and organise it?"

"It would be better if you went, for I do not see eye to eye with our parish priest, as you know. I had some altercation with him and since then we do not really get on. I leave it all to you."

"Well, all right then, let it be so."

"Goodbye then!"

"Goodbye, Mika! Do call a little more often," Marta urged him.

"Do call!" said Joza, getting up from his seat.

As soon as Mika left, Godmother Manda arrived all wrapped up in a large black shawl. Marta immediately greeted her, extending her arms towards her, as if asking for a great favour. She rolled her eyes and waved her arms about, as if the greatest possible misfortune that could befall a human being was on her head.

"Where have you been? I have not seen you for so long and here I will be going out of my mind if things carry on like that!"

Godmother Manda folded her arms across her chest, asking somewhat surprised:

"For God's sake, what is the matter? What has happened again? Tell me quickly, let me hear, let me know."

"And everything has fallen on my head as if I were damned," bemoaned Marta.

Joza was standing nearby and his face showed that he did not know what Marta was talking about.

"And what is that about?" asked Joza in a hoarse voice.

"There, I am telling you. The shameless hussy, she is no daughter of mine! A little while ago I came into the room and I saw it immediately. Mika was standing there in silence and I knew at once that something had happened. I went to look for her, to see where she had got to and I found her in her room. She had buried her nose into the pillow and was snivelling – I hope she never stops! I do not know exactly what happened but I can imagine, because she told me that she had said to his face that everything was over and he should leave her well alone! Is this the way to receive a young man who is serious about her and who does his best to ignore all her nonsense? Does that not prove that he is a generous and honest man? Can we or may we bear him a grudge? Had it been anybody else, he would not have looked at her again even if the whole region of Bachka had been hers!"

"Enough! I've had enough!"

Joza bellowed furiously, punching the table with his fist, causing a loud bang and things to fall off the table. The flame of the candle bent, almost to its extinguishing point. Had Marta not quickly caught the candle, it too would have fallen to the floor.

Joza yelled angrily and cursed so terribly that Godmother Manda was horrified:

"I have had enough!" he exclaimed. "There in the field that 'beggar' attacked me, he attacked me like a bandit, he nearly throttled me, and now she is up to no good. Bring her here! Bring her here so I can tear her into little pieces and throw them to the dogs, since she is not like the rest of the world, she does not obey her father who cared for her all those years, who treated her as the apple of his eye, supported her tenderly and spoilt her! Now, what I have lived to see! She exposes me to the mockery of the whole village, makes me and our house the laughing stock of the village! That's my thanks! That's my thanks for raising her, for making sure she marries into a good and wealthy house, so that after my death she will not be forced to go from pillar to post! That's my thanks now! Great thanks indeed! You scrimp, you save, you deny yourself in order to provide for her, for her to have a better life, and what does she do? She shamelessly spits in my face!"

Godmother Manda, pacifying them and taking Marta by the hands, said:

"For God's sake, if you are God-fearing people, let me come in for a moment! Calm down and stop cursing, because everything will end well. I will speak with her, I will settle everything with her, just leave her to me. Otherwise it will only get worse, seeing how you are acting now. Let's have some peace, we do not want the whole street to hear us, because even walls have ears nowadays – you say a word today and tomorrow the whole village knows about it, as if you trumpeted it."

"I do not want to see her, she makes my blood boil! I do not want to see her!" Joza continued to yell, pacing restlessly up and down the room.

Then he started coughing, heavily and painfully, for a long time, his face reddening and eyes bulging and becoming bloodshot, and his chest caving in and heaving:

"Is it not enough that I am ill? Does she have to embitter the days left of my old age instead of nursing me and cheering me up?"

He went to the adjoining room, shut the door behind him and was pacing backwards and forwards in the room for a long time, until he finally calmed down a little and went to bed without supper.

Godmother Manda took hold of Marta's hand, peered into her face and said in a whisper:

"Calm down! I understand how it is. Just leave it to me. It is not necessary to blow up immediately as you two have been doing. Perhaps a gentle way would be better. A kind word can open even iron doors. Anyway, it is worth trying. Just leave it to me. I will have a word with her now. Do not worry about it."

Godmother Manda left the room and went towards Shana's room. She paused at its door and listened. The room was in total darkness and so nothing could be seen. All she could hear was the intermittent sighing and rustling of a pillow, then quietness descended on the room and all around.

"Shana!" Godmother Manda called out in a gentle voice. The sound of her voice vibrated in the semi-darkness, vibrated and died out, but there was no answer. Only a sigh and rustling.

"Shana, my child, are you here? Here, I have come to see you."

"I am here," responded Shana. "Is it you, Godmother Manda?"

"It is me, my sweet child. Who else could it be! I have come to see you and you are here in the darkness. You are lying down, my darling, are you perhaps ill, unwell?"

Marta brought a candle into the room, placing it on the bedside table and leaving immediately. Pale reddish light spread out timidly around the walls, and across the bed on which Shana lay fully dressed with her head buried in the pillow.

Her godmother sat down on the chair near the bed and, caressing Shana's hair, she said:

"You have to look after yourself. Your health is always the most important thing. As long as you are healthy, your life is good, but once you fall ill, it is better not to be alive. I know this from experience."

Shana did not lift her head from the pillow. She did not respond to her godmother's words. Her hair fell over shoulders that began to tremble and rise as her head began to shake, and a quiet stifled cry rose to Godmother Manda's ears. She took hold of Shana's shoulders with both hands:

"Shana, my darling, why are you weeping? Tell me, child, tell me! Confide in me, I will understand you, because I went through much myself, I know how it is when one is suffering. Tell your Godmother Manda, she will understand you and help you."

Her hands caressed Shana's thick scented hair, ruffling it, and then she moved them to her white neck. In the bedroom, the oil-lamp was burning in a tired way. At the door, the darkness lay.

Shana raised her head and, turning around, she looked at Godmother Manda. Shana's large and deep eyes, that were once so full of the joys of spring and a carefree happiness, were now dimmed, full of tears, the thin wrinkles beneath her eyes leaving deep shadows, which now, in the light of the candle, seemed to be marked with gloom and an incurable sadness. Godmother Manda looked at her very carefully. A thought flashed through her mind: this was no longer the same Shana as she once was, a charming and naïve little girl, who always met her at the door to the street; she was no longer a carefree child who believed that everything her elders told her was the truth. She looked at Shana intently and she clearly saw that before her stood a different Shana, a young woman who could no longer be hoodwinked and silenced with false promises, that here was a young woman aware of herself and her feelings. She wanted to say something to Shana, but the words stuck in her throat. She cast her eyes down and a light sigh escaped, as if stealing from her bosom.

Shana's godmother began thoughtfully:

"And what can you do, my child! That is the way of life. I myself did not fare better in my youth. Almost all of us have gone through similar experiences. Maybe that's how it has to be. My head was filled with so many things at that time! And today when I think about it, it seems like a faraway dream that I was allowed to dream, but which could never be realised. At times I thought about it as something ridiculous, but also beautiful and exalted. My child, life is one thing, and what we want and hope for is another. We are all born to live, to work, to struggle and to deny ourselves, because that is life. We all have to yield to life and its laws, because it is merciless and takes no notice of our sighs and our tears. We daydream, building castles in the air, endlessly, whilst life drags us into this everyday reality, which can never satisfy us entirely. You can trust me, for I am no child, for I have experienced it all on my back. Indeed, my child, I have experienced it all!"

"But if only you knew what goes on in my soul, if only you knew?"

Shana sighed:

"Well, I could do anything you wish, I would object to nothing, but *this* I cannot do. I am telling you, I can't. Just at the thought of having to give up my feelings, something rises up within me. My inner self becomes agitated and I can see that it is all in vain. Something subconscious, something deep inside me resists your wishes. You all tell me that I am wilful, you tell me that you cannot understand me, but I cannot understand you either when you press me so much. Is my sole reason on this earth to marry Mika, because he is rich and that he can have all rights over me? To obey him when I feel that this is my disaster, and not being able to close my eyes, giving myself to him, giving myself to him for that crust of bread, whilst my heart is feeling otherwise? For me it is not the crust of bread alone that is important, I cannot resign myself to this. In your eyes I am ridiculous, I look naïve to you, because almost all of you gave up your first love in the name of self-interest and a piece … a piece of butter-smeared bread, but inside your souls remains an emptiness! Why do you not try thinking about the fact that I will have to live with the one I marry, that I will have to bear both the good and the bad in the marriage, thus being answerable only to myself for what I do? Why is everyone thinking differently from me, why are you all shouting 'He is rich, lacking nothing at all'?"

Godmother Manda shifted in her chair:

"You are right," she said slowly. "You are right. It is exactly as you have said. I thought the same at that time, and for sure the others thought the same, but a different way of understanding life had been established in our midst, creating unwritten laws that we had to obey. We had to obey their laws if we wanted to live in their midst, if we did not want to be pilloried by their understanding of life, if we did not wish to serve as their laughing-stock! And what could we poor women do here? Whither could we go? Whither? When one grasps that there is nowhere to go, when one grasps that this is what life is like, then we come to terms with it and allow other things to run their course!"

"Oh no, no, that I cannot do! Godmother Manda, this is not honest! It means to do something, though we are aware it is not honest, just because that is how in our midst, in which we live, it is done! Is this not shameful, is this not humiliating to oneself? I cannot do that. Everything in me is revolting against this, everything tells me I also have my rights if I have duties!"

"You have your rights, you feel you have your rights, but often one has to give up his rights. One has to give them up if one does not want to be an exception, if one wants to please one's family and show one's gratitude for the good they have showered on one. You know very well yourself that all plants cannot grow in all soils. They develop well in one kind of soil, it is a joy to watch them, but in another kind they wither, die, or barely survive from day to day. It is the same with people. Not every man is happy with the world he has to live in. He does not find in it that which his heart desires. His heart pines until he himself realises that his situation could be remedied. A plant cannot help itself, but a man himself can. This happens only when he realises that it is not a good idea to ponder on thoughts and feelings which make us unhappy, when he starts looking at life around him with more sober eyes, when he comes to terms with the demands of the world in which he lives. And if he does not make peace, then his life will certainly be a hard one!"

"So what has that got to do with me? I will either live as a human being should live, or not at all. I am telling you: *or not at all!* I cannot allow myself to be sold, I will not permit it, no matter what happens to me. And for this reason, I want you all to leave me alone. Stop torturing me with your advice and expressions of love that only boil down to me denying myself in order to go with the flow of the murky and filthy stream of the life of our village. I told him never to come before my eyes, because I cannot bear to look at him. I said that to his face. Where is his male pride!"

"To whom did you say this?"

The dry and harsh voice of Shana's mother was heard from the door.

"To Mika."

"What business do you have to say that to him? What business? You miserable wretch! Is that how you obey your mother, how you honour her care and her wakeful nights, whilst bringing you up? Shame on you! I've had enough. I am sick of your foolishness. I cannot take any more of this. It has to end. Start thinking! You know that on Sunday your banns are to be read in church for the first time!"

"They will not!" Shana shouted, terrified. "I will not have my banns read with anybody."

"This is our will and we shall take no notice of your silliness. You have to obey when you are asked!"

"In this case I cannot obey!"

"You have to!"

"Never!"

"Then get out of my house, go into the wide world, out of my sight, and don't you dare say to anybody that you are my daughter! Get out, get lost, out of my sight! You shameless hussy!"

Shana's eyes opened wide, as if taking in the verdict of her mother's words, filling her with an absolute and heavy darkness. Her chest began to heave and, as her mother's words became clearer to her, everything inside her became murky, and a crushing, immense pain pressed her bosom threatening to suffocate her. She saw nothing before her and everything spinning, everything blurring and floating before her as in a dream, as in a delirium. Suddenly, as if something strong and firm within her had broken and shattered, she recognised the light of the oil-lamp. A cold and deadly peace flooded her inner self, and indifference and acceptance of something unexpected filled her and stiffened her, so that she stared before her for a time without thought or feeling. Then she slowly got up and, without a word and without a sigh, she went to the door like a sleep-walker.

Godmother Manda watched, frightened. She wondered what had happened to Shana and what had suddenly entered her mind.

At the door, Marta stood in front of Shana and took her hand:

"Where are you off to?"

"I am going," said Shana icily, her face expressing utter stiffness.

"Where to?"

"I do not know. It does not matter. I am going somewhere where there are no people with their love which tramples and curses us."

"You fool! Are you raving? Have you gone mad? What the devil is wrong with you?"

"I can no longer stay here. I can't. It is finished! It is over and I must go. Leave me: I must go. I have nobody here any longer. I thank you for everything you have done for me, thank you for everything, but now I must go."

Godmother Manda started sobbing, her eyes filling with tears. Marta stood pale and surprised at the door, holding Shana's hand. At first she was afraid that Shana had gone mad and the thought horrified her. Terrified, she stared first at Shana and then at Godmother Manda. She had no idea what to do.

Silence fell in the room. Outside lay a thick darkness. The wind roared over the houses, shaking the branches of the mulberry trees. Somewhere in the distance a dog barked furiously, and the muffled sound of a song, as if severed, reached them.

Godmother Manda got up and came close to Shana. She laid her hands on her shoulders, and turning her towards herself she embraced her with tears in her eyes.

Sobbing, Godmother Manda said:

"Shana! Shana! Dear child, we love you and wish you well! You are our child, you are ours and we wish you well. And if you cannot marry him, stay here, after all you are ours!"

Shana's hands trembled, her fragile shoulders jerked and the frozen darkness in her soul began to melt as a light began to enter her heart.

She firmly embraced Godmother Manda as a drowning creature would grasp a straw and, breaking into heart-rending sobbing, she cried out:

"Save me, save me! I beg you."

Floods of tears flowed down her pale cheeks, whilst Marta stood at the door, looking with incomprehension at this unexpected scene ...

Chapter 12

That evening Mika went home in a discontented mood. As he was walking along the street that was inundated with a damp and suffocating darkness, he felt a certain unease settling in his soul, which pained him and pressed upon him with its icy, creepy hands. Wading through the soft, sticky mud, he pondered on all the things that had happened to him that evening. Shana was constantly before his eyes. He saw her beautifully shaped lips, her dainty marble-like white teeth, seeing her deep, sad eyes that looked at him with scorn, disparagingly. So far he had felt at ease thinking that Shana was just like many other girls in the village and that it would be easy for him to manage her, but now he began to feel disquiet and a sense of the humiliation that had just befallen him. He was not great in her eyes, he did not in any way cause her to admire him, he could not win her heart, she did not love him and today she had told him so to his face. This declaration caused him pain, sharp great pain, which suddenly changed his demeanour, and so his gaze fell to the ground. He realised that she was in another world, inaccessible to him, a world he could not enter, no matter how rich, wanton and proud he would be. They were not on the same level and he could find no way of crossing closer to Shana.

At the crossroads he stopped and raised his head, looking at the streets as if to take them all in. He was bleary-eyed, his thoughts uncertain, and not one could satisfy him. None could be relied upon, none could bring him the certainty that everything was going to be successful. At this moment all his wealth seemed to him insignificant and worthless, and in spite of all his pride and self-confidence that he was above everyone else in the village, he felt abandoned and alone. He realised that not everybody thought in the same way about the worthiness of man, as he himself thought, and as almost all the village thought.

So far, he had made conquests of the village girls on account of his wealth, and all of them enthused about the hope of a carefree and luxurious life but not one enthused about him as a man.

Suddenly he thought:

"If I were a poor man and owned nothing under God's blessed sky, working as somebody else's servant or like Marin who looks after sheep, would anybody remember me, would anybody even want to approach me or say a word of praise to me?"

So he asked himself why it was that Shana did not want him, that she could not stand the sight of him, that she simply wanted him out, feeling uncomfortable in his company. What were the reasons for this?

The darkness was becoming thicker, and was settling in his soul too. He felt a turbulence within, as if something was falling apart and that he would be dragged along with it, but it was not yet clear to him what this was. He surmised that not all men and women lived on the bread they ate, that not all could be satisfied with the same hopes, but that there was a worth within a human being that raised him above wealth, above any position in society, which had nothing to do with wealth. But he could not yet grasp this, because he had never heard about this inner worth from anybody in the village; nobody had ever spoken to him about it, nor had anybody attached any importance to it. It was precisely this vagueness and lack of clarity that troubled him the most, forcing him to think about himself. He could not do this as he did not know how to, because he lived in a world where it was not customary to think deeper with one's head than the level of how to live the life of small unimportant people, whose whole existence centred on the question of how to earn daily bread, how to secure the provisions for winter, and how to cut wood for fuel on the sly without being caught. Nobody had taught him to think any other way. Aside from the thoughts of a crude life, people were not clear about other ways of thinking; for them, they appeared to be dark birds that occasionally circled above them, but whose flights never stirred them into fully awakening to life. They were born on this land, born on this dark and damp soil, which fed them and caressed them, and for that reason they were its most faithful servants and slaves, because if they were removed from it, they would wilt and become lost. So this land was their life and hope, and they could not leave it. But those weighty questions of man and his meaning were usually solved with superstition. True enough, they believed (many did not) in God, but God was for them an old man with a long white beard, who sat in heaven to deal with their murky and selfish business, to send them rain in time of drought, and to give them an abundant and contented life. To be sure, there were those who sincerely entrusted themselves to God only when disaster befell them, they remembered Him then, but in good times they cursed Him, reviled Him, and spitting at anything sacred. They swore by God to defend their filthy undertakings; then they praised Him in order to derive some profit. They knew very little about the true God; though some did, those whose hearts were humble and whose souls were refined.

Mika was aware of this mixture in the village, but he did not get involved in its meaning, nor did he ever feel the need to do so. However, today he felt that life was not as he imagined it to be. He realised that not all people bowed before wealth or valued the man just because of it, but that there was contentment and happiness to be had without this abundance, without riches.

And he thought: Marin was a hired hand, working for somebody else to earn his keep as a poor man, and he was not thought of as a good catch in the village, whilst he, Mika, was held in esteem as the first in the village. In spite of these things, Marin beat him, he was taller than Mika, and Shana loved him! This knowledge caused Mika terrible torment. His face darkened, his eyes were bewildered, and his head hung low.

For a long time he wandered aimlessly through the streets and for the first time in his life he started thinking about man and his worth, which began to reveal itself to him. He arrived home in a sullen, bad-tempered mood and found his mother huddled up, sitting near the stove. The oil-lamp cast a sombre light over the inside of the room.

When he entered she slowly got up and stood before him, asking him in a quiet voice:

"Do you want your supper?"

For a while he stared as if thinking about something and then he sat at the table, holding his head in his palms, and said:

"What have you got for supper?"

She went to the little cupboard.

"I have already eaten but I left some meat and cakes for you. I waited for you, but when I got fed up with waiting, I sat down and I ate. I thought you would eat when you came back. Had I known that you would come, I would have waited."

"It does not matter. Give me the food," said Mika, sitting down at the table and raising the wick in the oil-lamp.

His mother brought him the food and she sat down in her previous place.

She stared at the floor whilst Mika ate without appetite and then, as if remembering something, she suddenly raised her head and said:

"Have you been to the Council Office today?"

Mika pushed his plate away and looked at her, wiping his mouth:

"I haven't."

"Did not the local taxman find you either?"

"No. Why?"

"He was here looking for you."

"What did he want? Did he say?"

"He brought a note. I don't know how to read it. He said something about some tax owing, something like that. He left the note, asking me to give him five dinars. I did not give him the money. Where would I get five dinars from?"

"Where is this note?"

"Here!"

Mika had a good look at the note and his face scowled. He threw it away and shouted angrily:

"Who the hell can pay so much tax? I paid the tax not so long ago and here they are again demanding the rest! Every day they want this and that. Who can pay all this? Today you pay them all they ask for and tomorrow they want some more arrears. They would be satisfied only if you sold all your miserly property and gave them what they asked for. It is always give, give, and what use is this local authority to us?"

Mika paced the room angrily. In his mind's eye, he saw the Notary Public, who was rumoured to be a trained barber, and God alone knows by whose protection he became Notary Public. And now, as he was stuck up, he considered himself one of the intelligentsia, with a wife, a fancy chatterbox, on his arm, and everybody greeting them with a bow, addressing him as Mister Notary Public! What enraged Mika the most was the gossip which said that this Notary Public must be very clever and wily, and that he did not need any education. If it had not been so, he would not have attained this honour.

Mika was roused from his reverie by a knocking on the door, which opened immediately, and their neighbour Reza, a good friend of Mika's mother, entered. Reza was the one who secretly traded in second-hand worn-out suits and she was the one who had received more beatings than hot dinners from her husband whilst he was still alive, due to her zealous honesty and over-active tongue: her mouth was always stuffed with more words than soup. Hardly getting through the door she started babbling in her sharp, quick tongue, running towards Mika's mother and asking her about her health and about everything that had happened since they last saw each other, which was yesterday at the same time. She complained of stomach pains and of the cold she had caught yesterday whilst washing clothes at the well, and she explained that she called now just for a few moments, since she saw the candle still burning and thinking they were not ready for bed yet. Finally, she added that she also came because she had heard about something that Mika, and Jela his mother, would certainly find very interesting, and which would benefit them.

"And what is this news?"

Mika's mother's curiosity was roused and she sat closer to Reza, who pulled closer the ends of her shawl that she had tied round her middle.

"It is rumoured, many rumours in the village, that your Mika is going to be married. All the village is talking about it. But as I listen I begin to think that perhaps it is not so, because you cannot always believe what the world says. Often people invent things you could not even dream about. And I, then, in order to convince myself of the veracity of the rumours, I have come to tell you about what I have heard. After all, you are his mother, you would know best."

"And what is it I would know, Reza?"

"Indeed, who would if you didn't? Who else would know, if not you?"

"It is up to Mika. He knows best. Mika decides what will be. I do not interfere in these matters. He can do what he thinks best, you make your own luck."

Reza looked at Mika, shaking her head as if to scold him jokingly:

"Why are you keeping quiet like a tomcat, you great big fellow? What sort of a young man are you that you fail to boast about getting married? And about inviting me to the wedding so I can sing and dance to my heart's content, as I have not done in ages? You found a beautiful young woman too. She is rich, that is most important. And you have a right to marry. What is the point of waiting any longer? You are in your prime. What is the point of having a wife when you are older? Just to be looked after and nursed? Marry whilst you are young!"

Rezika carried on in this manner with her quick tongue for a long while, but she could get nothing out of Mika and she began to feel insulted. He sat in the chair, bowed down, and it seemed that he heard nothing of what Rezika was saying. His body was present but God knows where his thoughts were.

Suddenly he got up, pushed his hands in his pockets and walked to and fro in the room with his head still bowed. Then he stopped by the window, looked out into the darkness, and surveyed the room, abruptly leaving without a word. Reza watched him go in surprise, and when he slammed the door she directed a questioning look at Jela, as if looking for an explanation for Mika's behaviour. She did not understand this, because she knew Mika as a roguish and rakish young man, who left no one alone and who teased all the girls and younger women.

Therefore, she spoke to Jela in an important and caring tone:

"What's up with him, woman?"

"I do not know," Jela shrugged her shoulders.

"Since when has he become like that?"

"I do not know. I have recently noticed a great change in him and he really does not look like his old Mika. Only God knows what's eating him."

"Where has he gone now?"

"How would I know? He never says what he is up to or what he thinks. He comes home, sits down, paces the room, eats, looks out of the window, thinks about something, and leaves. I can tell you nothing else. I dare not even ask him, because when long ago I asked him what was wrong, he yelled at me to leave him alone because he was tired and had enough problems of his own."

"That is not good."

"Well, I always sit here at home alone like a prisoner or go into the garden and that is all I have. I suffer, what else can I do! Maybe that is my fate. He is estranged from me, rarely does he speak to me, he does not ask me for anything, like other sons do; he does not ask me how I am, what I do, or if I need anything. So I keep quiet, suffer and grieve. That is my life, dear friend. So many times I have wept through sorrow or grief for wilting here like a neglected tree. On Sunday I visit the grave of my old man, weeping and grieving there. When I come home I feel easier and less depressed. I pray to God to take pity on me and take me, since I am of no use to anyone. If you did not come every now and then to see me and check how I am doing, I would not know that there is anybody alive around me. Am I such a sinner that God punishes me like that?"

Reza listened carefully to her and approved all her words by nodding her head, showing to her that she understood Jela's predicament and that she felt sorry for her.

She took her hands and said:

"I think I know what is wrong with him and why he acts as he does."

"Tell me if you know. At least I will hear it from you, since I cannot learn anything from him."

"There is talk in the village, as you know people know all sorts of things, and there is talk that Shana is humiliating him and cheating on him. She is cheating on him, the hussy. They say that she was seen at night meeting Marin, that cripple. I am sure this must be painful for Mika. And why not indeed, my dear, he is after all the most desirable man in the village, since he is famed for his good looks. And now here comes a big oaf and bumpkin to spoil his chances."

"Shana is cheating on Mika?" asked Jela incredulously.

"On him, my dear."

"And what has she to do with my Mika?"

"Do you not know that Mika visits them at home and that it had already been agreed that Shana would marry Mika?"

"Who agreed? Who made the agreement?"

"Do you really not know anything?" Reza said in surprise and shock.

"I do not know anything. Nobody has spoken to me about it. Now is the first time I hear it, from you."

"Well, the whole village knows about it, and you do not know? Mika has already arranged everything with Joza and all that needs to be done now is to name the date for the wedding."

"Really?" Jela said thoughtfully, lowering her eyes. "I know nothing about all this. What can one do, I am only his mother and he can be forgiven for not telling me anything. Oh, what have I lived to see in my old age, what has befallen the poor woman I am that even my son has forgotten me, he no longer respects me! And when I think back to how I cared for him, how I nurtured him right from infancy, how I brought him up, how I always saved the best piece of food for him. And how he treats me now, as if I were not his mother at all."

Her worn-out old hands fell helplessly into her lap, her fingers absent-mindedly caressing the rough cloth of the frock that she was wearing. In her soul began to appear something from far away, quietly, softly, slowly rising into her bosom, as if wanting to free itself and soar into the heights. Those wrinkled and wizened and dried-up cheeks of hers, on which time had left a deep mark, looked even more wrinkled and took on a grey hue. Her eyes, dimmed with age, were filled with bitter maternal tears that flowed forlornly and flowed slowly down her worn-out sheepskin jacket.

"Oh, my God, what else will I live to see yet!" she sighed, looking pensively before her.

Rezika moved away and became worried, herself.

"I thought you knew all about this. The whole village is agog with the news. But they also say that Shana does not care a hoot for Mika, that she avoids him! You as a mother should know about all of this, he should have told you everything, because where should a child go to confide if not to his mother?"

When Jela found herself alone she laid her head in her hands and wept loudly and bitterly. All the sorrow, all the loneliness, and all the heavy weight that fell on her shoulders after her husband's death, all the grief and self-denial, all this flowed into her now and seized her powerfully and mercilessly, breaking her heart, tearing her soul apart. She was hurt by everything that Reza said. Her every word was like a sword to her heart, her every word harder to bear than any curse or contempt. She sat thus with her head in her hands for a long time and thought about her past; a past that consisted of much worry and suffering and so little of joy; so little of understanding. Since she found so little understanding from her husband, because she married him against her will, according to the demands of her parents, she had hoped that her child would understand her and that he would be the joy, consolation and support of her old age, but now she could see that she had been left to herself and she would continue to live her own inner life as she had lived it first in her youth, and then as a young woman and then as a mother. And now, as she looked back on her past life and asked herself what she had wanted from life and what she had hoped for, comparing it with what had actually happened, she realised that all her dreams had remained only dreams, and that she would carry them to her cold grave; that her life had been bitter and unbearable, because she had never been understood.

On the hard wooden table the oil-lamp continued to burn, with its flickering reddish and murky light: somewhat like the light those closest to her had offered her all her life.

She knew very well that land was much more appreciated than a human being; that an animal, when sick, received more care and better attention than a human being. All her life she had suffered, right from her childhood, but she could not complain about it to anyone. She was rich and had married into a rich house; but happy, she was not: wealth did not make her happy. All she knew was that she had suffered a lot and worked very hard, but that the real life, which she had had only glimpses of, continued to pass her by.

Mika returned home late at night and found her sitting there deep in thought and troubled. That surprised him. It was not her habit to sit late into the night or be working at something, as she always went to bed fairly early. And when he noticed her tear-stained eyes and how forlornly she sat, as if in some other world not known to him, he came close to her and placed his hand on her shoulder – for the first time in a few years. But she did not raise her head. She continued to stare before her, not moving at all.

Mika shook her shoulder and said:

"What is the matter with you? Are you perhaps ill?"

She laughed bitterly and looked at him desolately:

"It would be better to be ill than what has happened to me."

Mika scowled.

"What has happened to you?"

"It is rather sad, my son, to hear things from other people that I should have known in the first place. It is sad enough."

"It is probably that nattering gossip Rezika who barked a lot of nonsense and filled your ears with God knows what. I dare her to ever again cross my threshold!"

"I never even dreamt that I would live to see this."

Mika paced the room impatiently.

"Come on, say it, what have you lived to see?"

"If you had asked me for advice and listened to me, this would not have happened."

"What would not have happened?"

"This: that the whole village is laughing at you. You think yourself so fine and clever, that nobody is your equal in the whole world, and there is that common village slut, who doesn't care as long as there is a man. And you want to take her for your wife, to bring her here into the house so my old head would have to see what this shameless hussy would be doing, disgracing me and pushing me into an early grave? Now I know why you never said a word about her, and why you hid everything from me and did as you pleased! Are there no good girls in the village? Is she your match? But it is always like that when the mother has not been obeyed!"

Mika stopped in the middle of the room. At first her words surprised him. They surprised him, and then acutely and mercilessly they pierced his heart.

"And what was there to tell when I did not know that anything would come of it? But today when I know how things are, I am telling you I will get married and bring Shana into this house: in spite of all of them, however many there are, even where they stand on their heads!"

"You would bring her into this house? Oh …!"

"Her!"

"It would be better for me not to exist! It would have been better if I had given birth to a stone. At least I would not have this terrible disgrace inflicted upon the house! Are you not ashamed in front of the honest folk who will point their fingers at you, saying: 'Look at him now, he thought himself clever and wise, and now he takes for himself a wife who behaved so shamelessly with Marin?' Is she your match now? She, who avoids you and says she cannot stand the sight of you! What wonderful things I have lived to see!"

Mika angrily paced the room. His cheeks were red. His inner self became unsettled and turbulent. He searched for a thought that could explain to his mother the whole situation, but he found none. He was becoming increasingly angry, because his mother's words told him that she too knew that Marin had got the better of him. He had been disgraced and the best thing for him now was to hang his head in shame and retreat. Why should he retreat? And before whom? So that they could pillory him at any opportunity: "Indeed," he thought to himself, "why did you not take Shana for your wife when you are the best? Now you will take one that others can take?"

To him, it seemed already that he could see a multitude of mocking faces, the small envious eyes of which derision glistened restlessly and sneeringly. He already heard all around him the laughter and mocking voices that followed him at every step and would not leave him. And in his mind, these glistening, envious, flashing eyes, and those mocking voices in his subconscious, irritated him and carried him on a powerful wave of rage.

"No, I will not retreat, not for anybody's sake, they can all croak like an animal, drop dead with rage, but Shana must be mine, no matter what! I am telling you this loud and clear, so you will know and you will not be able to tell me later that I have kept you in the dark. This very autumn I will bring Shana into this house and I will muzzle everyone's mouths, I will throw dust in their eyes, and they will know that she will be mine and mine alone, as long as I shall live."

He turned round and slammed the door behind him. The only thing he could hear from the room was his mother's weeping and he had a vision, as if through a mist, of her frightened, distorted, feverish and crushed face.

Outside, the night was very dark. A profound and heavy darkness lay over the small village houses that were huddled closely together as if afraid of witches, werewolves and the dead: all the things that were talked about during the long winter evenings. No sound came from anywhere. The sky was turbid and cloudy, and the raw air lay over the yards, gardens and fields, as if trying to fill the sapless bosom of the earth that was at last eager for rest and tranquillity with its vital juices.

Mika walked around the yard nervously. He wanted to go, somewhere far away, where he could find his lost peace. Finally, he entered his room, threw himself on the bed without undressing, placed his hands under his head, closed his eyes and sighed heavily. Before his eyes, appeared the scene with Shana. In his head, he heard her words to leave her alone, not to persecute her. So then he himself thought that it would be best if he did leave her alone, never crossing the threshold of her home again. He himself wanted it, but he could not do it. There was something stronger within him that was stronger than himself, something that drew him to Shana, that bound him to her. The more he thought of leaving her, the more he realised that he could no longer live without her, that he needed her.

He turned over on his side and buried his face in the pillows. Grabbing hold of his head, he shook it in desperation. He had never experienced feelings like this. He had never suffered so much in respect of a girl as now. He was angry with himself for being such a weakling, for not being able to stop thinking about her. How he longed to have her love him, as she loved Marin! He would feel so differently in his heart! But he could feel that she hated him and this hurt him. It hurt knowing that she was given to him in marriage because of his wealth, that she was given against her will.

She will come, she will, because she will have to come; and he will show everybody that Shana is here in his house, that she is his wife, though he will be tortured by the knowledge that Shana's heart is not his and that between them stands an abyss which he would never be able, with any amount of money, to breach. In this respect, his wealth was totally useless, because even her parents' power stopped there! But who in the village would even think about that? Who would even bother to think that Shana was not his?

Chapter 13

Six days a week people worked hard, six days from morning to night they toiled and worked and cared, and on the seventh day the sun rose from the east and Sunday came. Sunday came, composed and festive over the distant valleys, waters and woods, crossing in every way the fields, all the paths in the hollows, and arriving early whilst children were still asleep. It came to the village to encourage people and creatures towards a new life. Although it was autumn, when the days were usually murky and rainy, windy and cold, Sunday was almost always filled with sunshine and infused with freshness and young life. This gladdened the people, land, and animals alike. Today, the cattleman's horn echoed more pleasantly and more beautifully along the streets, its sound overflowing clearly and mischievously, a consequently unobtrusive and pure sound. Even the cows' mooing was somehow different from usual. A new breath of serenity, tranquillity and of surrender filled this Sunday morning, a renewed faith and hope flowing into men's thoughts and an incredible joy flooding the inner souls of human beings, who this morning unconsciously became aware of the power of life that nurtured, fed and upheld them. In the clean large sheds over the mangers full of hay, horses neighed restlessly, shaking their long loose manes. In the yard, ducks milled around and hens flew down from the mulberry trees, hurrying to pick up the maize grain that the housewives had scattered in the early morning. However, the joy of this Sunday morning did not enter all houses equally. The sunny fingers of Sunday joy knocked carefully on every door, though many doors failed to open and many a heart remained cold, tight and empty.

To Joza's house also, Sunday brought no serenity, no lightheartedness, nor the joy of the Lord's day. The sun scattered no intimate feelings of home life under his eaves. Neither the sun nor joy entered Joza's house. A cold, rigid peace lay over the beautifully furnished rooms, whilst melancholy and dejection rested on Shana's face. Her eyes flitted frantically from object to object. Because of the suffering of her soul, she did not feel that Sunday had arrived. She saw the sunshine in the yard, she heard the cattleman's horn and the mooing of the cows, but joy did not enter her soul. Now she had nothing beautiful to hope for, as in the past when she used to hurry to the circle-dance immediately after the afternoon light meal, to squeal and surrender herself to the merry vortex of her youth.

Joza had left in the early morning to go somewhere in the village, having said nothing to anyone; Marta was kindling the fire in order to finish cooking the meal; and then, as soon as the big bell rang for high Mass, she would put on her Sunday best and go to church. The flames crackled under the pots, and smoke rose and twisted, making its way into the sooty neck of the chimney, whilst Shana did some tidying in the room.

Outside, in the street, children stood around in their new and clean clothes, but they did not play as they usually did on weekdays: instead, they watched and stealthily assessed whose suits and jacket buttons were the nicest. The children became more serious as they walked along the main street that was wide and covered in gravel, and which led from the cemetery to the church. Women passed beneath the windows, dressed all in black, their heads covered in black scarves. Others were still wearing the light-coloured clothes and multi-coloured dainty slippers that gaped and knocked against their heels. Maidens were bareheaded with paper flowers in their hair, rouge tinting their cheeks and full lips. Men were smoking pipes or cigarettes, pensively blowing the smoke away over and over, having serious discussions about their business affairs and their worries about the taxes that were draining the life out of them and sucking their bones.

They also discussed politics, making plans for new elections, talking about the better days that they expected from these elections. As they talked about these new days, more pleasant and better, they moved towards the district house and then, from there, at the sound of the second bell, they went into the church to pray to God. And these narrow streets, which during the week were usually empty with not a soul to be seen, were now lively and filled with humanity.

Shana watched the men and women and maidens and young men, and her chest tightened and she felt faint. She knew very well that all of them would be in the church today and they would hear the parish priest announcing her banns for the first time. All of them would hear it and their eyes would seek her out to feast on her.

She looked at the table standing near the wardrobe. Her new maiden's dress was laid out on it. Today she would wear it, and today their neighbour Marija would come to adorn her with flowers and tiny trembling mirrors, which would quiver on her head. Today her head would be "dressed to the nines", because she would be presented as a fiancée before the whole village. Looking at the dress and the flowers it seemed to her that none of this was for her, but to someone else, for some unknown girl. She remembered her maidenhood dreams, so full of joyful trepidation and anticipation of the day when she would become betrothed.

But now, now it was all so different. What hopes she had had, what dreams ... and now, what had befallen her! She had had to renounce everything, all hopes dashed, because life doesn't follow dreams, because life doesn't know mercy. She had had to renounce everything for the love of her parents, so they would not curse her later.

Their neighbour Marija arrived and dressed her and adorned her hair "full-head". How Marija marvelled at Shana, how she watched her with admiration! Shana's pale cheeks gave her the impression of thoughtfulness, self-possession, and pensiveness; and her dark, sad eyes spoke clearly of the profound and tremendous feelings that had been banished into the immeasurable distance.

The church bell rang, flooding the village with its sound, and entering the room where Shana stood before a large mirror. And Marta entered the room, dressed in her Sunday best, with her prayer book in her hand and the cloth that she used to kneel on in the church thrown over it.

"We should go, we do not want to be late!" she said, and went out. Shana bowed her head and followed.

The great warm sun had shone for so many years over this land, where it ripened the wheat, maize, vineyards and all other crops, the sun that gave life to everyone equally and unselfishly. This very sun, even now, shone so joyfully and openly over the village, pouring its light over the paths and the well-trodden ways in front of the houses. Women poured forth, with stooping shoulders; maidens smiled joyfully and turned round to see if they could spot their young men; and men hurried to get to church as soon as possible. Shana, with her head bowed, walked beside her mother and felt no warmth from the life-giving sun, no joy at the laughter of the maidens nor at the playfulness of the innocent little children. Both women and maidens kept turning round, whispering confidences to one another; and the young men followed her with their restless eyes, laughing loudly. Sounds of brass-band instruments could be heard bold and sharp, followed by the village firemen dressed in their ceremonial uniforms with their heads held high. The sun abundantly bestowed on them its fiery rays, which reflected from their copper helmets and blazed up in a triple glow of celebration and boldness. This band of firemen were followed by a multitude of inquisitive and enthusiastic children, who hopped and skipped from side to side, totally surrendering to the sound of the music. Today the firemen had a celebration of their own, so already from the early morning they were gathering and ready to go. They all went towards the church, where people were congregated under the large and well-branched trees growing right against the fence of the parish priest's garden. Some people stood near the large stone cross in front of the church door, talking about matters that had taken place in the last few days. The women, on the other hand, immediately entered the church, dipping their wrinkled and bent fingers into the water fonts, crossing themselves; they then went to sit down in the pews and on the stone in the middle of the church, or at the sides placing their kneeling mats on the ground to make themselves more comfortable. There in front, right near the altar itself, was the place for maidens. Behind them, slightly lower and in front of a partition which was covered with white cloth, was the place for the young married women. These young women's heads were all covered in a multitude of colourful scarves, whilst the maidens were bare-headed. By the time Shana entered the church it was completely full and lit up by the warm rays of sunshine, streaming in obliquely through the large church windows. When she took her place with the maidens they all smiled kindly at her, and she responded with a forced smile. She immediately opened her expensive black leather-bound prayer book, wanting to immerse herself in prayer. Lower down behind her, like a large but leisurely wave, swayed the multitude of people who had come today to hear the word of God, and to find refreshment and support in these days of hardship and toil.

Above the sacristy door, the bell rang with its high-pitched chime. The organ, like the sound of water during a flood, roared amongst the multitude of mixed voices that suddenly filled the church and heralded the solemn beginning of God's service. The priest, with the altar boys, entered the church from the sacristy door and climbed to the altar. Behind him stood the young men who followed God's service from there.

Shana was engulfed by a warm shudder and it seemed to her that in the sound of the organ music and in the voices of the singers in the choir loft, she heard the song of her soul longing to soar in the heights and seeking inner light, just as these voices were rising and losing themselves in the depths of these people's souls, which in that moment were experiencing their wretchedness and smallness before the face of God.

As the sound of the organ quietened, assembled, and died under the vault, Shana looked into her prayer book, but the large letters floated before her eyes and she just could not collect her thoughts to pray calmly and humbly as she usually would.

In her soul appeared a deep and despairing voice that hurried with great strength to the altar, asking, "God, why have you forsaken me, when all the others had already forsaken me? At least You are able to understand me, since these people cannot understand me, because Your Kingdom is in our souls and not in this soil on which we are bartered for, tortured, and crucified on the cross. Is it not a greater sin, if, by obeying my parents, I give myself to the man I do not love so that he could crucify me, than the disobedience to my parents? Tell me what to do, enlighten my mind and fortify my heart with the light of the Holy Faith, that I may not lose heart, that I do not stray from the right path. Tell me, is it necessary for me to give up all the joys of this world, as You did Yourself, when You accepted the crown of thorns for Your divine head and the white shirt of a lunatic?"

And these thoughts filled her soul, rising from the deepest corners of her heart as a sincere and true confession, in which she sought life-giving medicine. But the large crucifix above the altar stood immobile, and on the face of the crucified Christ lay a bitter and painful spasm that froze into a hard, rigid flint. This figure floated before her eyes, speaking to her clearly of the misery, suffering and nailing on the cross of the greatest Truth that ever appeared amongst people. The priest faced the people, extending his arms, and sang: *"Dominus vobiscum!"*

His voice rose above the heads of the people, the voice full of pristine whiteness and solemnity, like white clouds floating over the fields on a spring morning, and from the choir many united voices responded with *"Et cum spiritu tuo!"*, as if wholeheartedly they had entrusted themselves to a great and powerful being.

Shana looked towards the door of the sacristy and thought she recognised Marin amongst the other young men. She shuddered to the depths of her soul, as if to freeze her. Then a powerful cry of immense longing began to rise within her, telling her to tear all the flowers from her hair and to leave everything, and to throw herself onto his chest.

Her gaze fell on the stone crucifix above the altar. The dead eyes of the Son of God gazed back at her and from his side flowed the warm, red blood. It seemed to her that a distant voice was telling her to restrain her heart, to accept the sacrifice, because man becomes greatest through suffering and self-denial. Let her sacrifice herself, because there would come a day when she would be triumphantly raised from suffering and when her head would be crowned with the wreath of victory. She bowed her head with her heart beating fast and furiously and her chest rising fitfully and quickly.

She dared not look at the door of the sacristy because she had a feeling that Marin's gaze was resting on her, full of pain and suffering, a gaze that clearly spoke of all the promises and all the hopes they had both nurtured. How could she now look into his eyes, when she allowed them to adorn her hair with flowers and mirrors, and when today the priest would pronounce her solemnly from the altar as the betrothed of the one who is bloody before her eyes and who would suck out her youth and her life. Thus, she could no longer raise her eyes and direct them towards the sacristy door, because she felt humiliated and dishonoured, and because in the depths of her soul she felt she had become an unfaithful, weak and conniving woman, like all the others who had walked the same path before her. Then she remembered the first evenings of their meetings, when the brushwood was in leaf, when the grass smelt so sweet, when near the brook the flock of white-fleeced sheep grazed, when the first dusk fell, enveloping the woods in the distance, the tall poplars and the reeds, just as she had begun to be drawn into a pleasant, restless and foreboding feeling and when, for the first time, she felt the joy and meaning of life. Everything passed before her eyes, coming and going, and she clasped her bosom, looking at her past as if at a good friend who was on the point of deserting her now, never to return again. A thought pierced her again with full force:

would it not be a greater sin before God's face to take an oath of fidelity to Mika, to say that she would take him for her husband of her own free will, when, quite consciously, she felt only disgust for him? Would this not be a greater sin than her disobedience to her parents? Would this union be holy before God and people, would God be pleased with this life, which His servant was going to bind on this earth, when she knew very well that her heart belonged to another? But she had to take Mika in order to live amongst the people, who would then consider her life with Mika an honest one, because they stuck blindly like a drunk to a fence to the visible formalities of the marriage contract.

The church was full of people.

The sun was shining through the large windows. Women were praying at the rear. They prayed to God for the grace to help them humble their neighbours, help them get wealthy, live in abundance. They prayed that envious and poor people would be consumed by this envy. Let God send misfortune and all sorts of disasters on the heads of these others. And when their own hens are broody, when from the bottom of their hearts they desire the death of their old parents, who are only in the way and a burden, and when they drink in secret and cheat on their husbands, may He be of help to them. And finally, after this life, which they had spent "being faithfully obedient and carrying out God's commandments", that they would be granted eternal life and the joy of heaven! Women and maidens prayed, married men prayed, and the young men at the sacristy door were pushing and winking at the maidens and joking amongst themselves. And from the choir loft the organ was booming and many voices were rising to the vault of the church. All of them came here bringing their wishes and requests, their pride, and their humility.

Shana had no time to think about the singing and about the whispering lips around her and from behind her. She stared before her and it seemed to her she had strayed amongst these people, who gathered in the church and humbly bowed their heads, as if they were the most faithful servants of God's commandments and defenders of the Kingdom of God. She began to feel suffocated and sick. She felt superfluous in their company and before the face of God. Suddenly a thought struck her and filled her soul with fear: "What are you looking for amongst this humanity where you don't find understanding, and why are you praying to the same God as these people who are the executioners of your freedom, who barter with your virginity? Get up and go far away from all of them, if you want to remain pure and free."

Her hand was squeezing her prayer book tightly, her fingers in spasm; her chest heaving heavily to the point of not being able to breathe. She slowly raised her right leg and as she was about to rise, as if awakening from a dream, she heard words from God's altar. A young, tall and pensive priest was speaking to the people about the greatness of God's deeds, about the joy of creation, the kingdom in their souls, which cannot be destroyed by misfortune, and about love, pure and great. Truly Shana paid all her attention to the priest's words, which he delivered firmly in a measured fashion:

"God created you in His image. He gave you a soul and a heart, because nothing in the world has greater value than the soul and the heart. He has given you love in order to ennoble you to be pure and decent, to protect it and not to buy it and sell it, as you trade your sheep, wheat and land. Because in your heart and in your soul there is the Kingdom of God, and the Kingdom of God is more precious than money. God gave you the land and breathed into it the life of begetting, of fecundity; he sent you the rain to water it and the sun to warm it. The land delivered you the fruit so that you may manage it justly according to God's commandments. You may buy and sell your wheat and wine, your sheep and maize, but you may not trade your honour, your soul, your heart. For you can price your own wheat, which is for your needs, but you cannot put a price on your soul, because the eternal will of God decreed that it shall be the path which will lead you to Him. The land with all its riches is temporal, but the soul of man is eternal. And I tell you, blessed are those who are not blinded by the earthly riches, who live according to the commandments of God, because they will live already on this earth as human beings and not as beasts. To man alone, God gave love that raises him above the beasts, which live according to their natural instincts. And if you destroy love in a man's heart, you extinguish in him a great and holy light that has been lit by the hand of the Almighty to guide your way, to console you, to help you to persevere in carrying the burden of this life. Blessed are those who love in the Lord, because they are the true emissaries of the Lord's fields, the creators of the Kingdom of God on earth. May Love unite you and uphold you, may its beauty reign in your hearts and you will not leave the path of righteousness. For loving hearts are generous and ready to sacrifice and all good is found in them, but the hearts without love are like the fruit trees without fruit, like the earth without the sun. The loveless hearts sow injustice, selfishness and evil! May you always keep before your eyes a pure and sincere love, that it may be the foundation of your hearths, may love be with you in your fields when you are at work, may it be a consolation during the days of difficulties and scarcity, and may it be a joy in the days of plenty and happiness. Great and deep is the human heart! Scientists can measure the heights of mountains and the depths of the oceans, but who can measure the human heart?"

The young priest spoke for a long time from the altar. His voice was warm and at times trembled like the grain stalks swaying in the wind, then it restlessly floated above the people's heads, as if about to weep over them. His eyes, full of warmth, shone with spiritual light over the souls who in that moment experienced all their baseness and injustice, all the filth of their ceaseless bartering. Oh, how wonderful and great looked now the young priest, who spoke of the love that the village betrayed. How lofty was this young priest who spoke about the value of the soul that failed to find a home in these human bodies. His voice filled the church with the great festive atmosphere, and the meaning of his words touched and melted many a heart.

Shana's face turned pale as she watched him. It seemed that his words were directed at her, that his words were calling to her not to despair, to keep going to the end, because only the one who fights the fight to the end gains a victory. She understood very well every word which touched her to the core and which was the last and only light in her soul. Her lips stopped moving. She prayed no longer. She no longer saw any of the humanity around her. And when the priest turned round again and announced in a calm and collected voice Shana and Mika's first banns, followed immediately by a boom from the organ, Shana grabbed hold of her neighbour to avoid falling to the floor.

"What is the matter with you, Shana?" her neighbour asked.

She did not respond. The maidens around her kept looking at each other and watching her with fear. Shana's face was as white as a sheet and her eyes had that faraway look. Upon looking more closely at her, they saw large tears trickling down her cheeks, but she neither moved nor attempted to use her handkerchief to wipe them away. A hymn rose from the choir loft and hundreds of voices sang in unison. Thus, whilst everyone was filled with enthusiasm and penitent festivity, in Shana's heart there was only ever-increasing darkness. Indeed, the very sound of the organ and the singing of the people seemed to her one big obscene lie that was glorified with the incense, the lie that inebriated these masses with its irascible and concupiscent odour.

In the depths of her being she felt that all this was hypocrisy and a flea-market gaudiness; all that lurked underneath was personal interest, the desire to make money and the desire to cheat. And if this life was really as revealed, if that inner light that she longed for truly was not to be found, why had this longing been implanted in her soul, why was everyone talking about justice, love and honesty, if they did not exist anywhere, when it was all a lie and a sham, concealing beneath only vileness, cynicism and the callous and godless dealing?

Whilst the sounds of the organ rang out, she realised that she had reneged on her promised word, she herself had taken this path of insincerity. She in her weakness had allowed herself to be betrothed to Mika in front of all these people. And what effect had all this had on Marin? What did he think of her now? She thought that he must despise her and be disgusted with her betrayal, her faithlessness. How he had always trusted her, how good he had always been, how he loved her! And what had she done? How had she repaid him? Darkness swamped her anew and her disquiet grew in intensity. She looked in the direction of the sacristy door in trepidation in case she spotted him, but he was no longer there. The place he had stood on was now empty. Where had he gone and what was he going to do? And if she came across him, how could she look him in the eye?

The maidens around her stood up.

The priest and the altar boys went to the sacristy. The people started leaving the church. Only the organ was still singing tirelessly, but the melody was sad and vague. When Shana arrived home, she sat on a chair cradling her head in her hand. A terrible emptiness filled her and a great indifference towards everything enveloped her.

"So this is the day of my betrothal? Is this how my hopes have been realised?"

And again, before her appeared all those dreams of the day of her joy, when she would be betrothed, when she would be getting married. And then her eyes darkened and it was obvious that in that moment, she had made a decision. She got up and looked at herself in the mirror. She caught sight of her pale face and her adorned head. For a few moments she stared at herself in the mirror. Then she grabbed the flowers from her hair and left them strewn on the floor. When her mother entered, she was surprised and asked her angrily what she was doing. Shana cast a cold and withering glance at her:

"I have had enough of this farce."

"What farce?"

"That's it. I have done my bit. It is more than I can take. If you want, you can adorn your head and have the banns announced for yourself and Mika, but leave me out of it. I'd rather do anything than marry Mika, who is bloody before my eyes. You have been poisoning and torturing me until today, but that is it, no more. I will not live like cattle with Mika, because I cannot bear him."

Marta set her arms akimbo and frowned upon Shana.

"So that is what you think, girl? You still have not come to your senses? You are still wasting time with all these nonsensical thoughts? That's not enough for you, because you want to shame our house before the whole world? And on this day, on this blessed day, you bring disquiet and sin into our house. Do you not fear God?"

"God does not wish or demand of me to marry a person whom my heart refuses. Did you not hear what the priest said in the church? If you did, then you know what he said."

"I heard, how could I not have heard! Do you think I was dozing in the church? That is his trade, his duty to speak like that. They all say one thing and do another."

"I see, yes. So this means nothing to you?"

"Nothing at all. I know what I have to do and don't you start telling your grandmother how to suck eggs. You are to stop this nonsense once and for all, and you will not commit sin in our house."

"I have no desire to commit sin in your house, but I do wish to have my rights acknowledged so that I know I am a christened soul. It cannot go on like this. How would you feel if you were forced to live with somebody repulsive to you? What sort of life would that be? With all due respect, and all the wealth, when in your soul you feel dissatisfaction ... And what sort of life would I have, when it would always remind me of the violence, when it would always remind me of my destroyed happiness? I am sure that God himself cannot demand from me what all of you are demanding. For God is just and does not care about how much land anybody owns. But for you, only the man who has money is good, clever and honest. To you, money is all. You would give anything for money. For the love of money you want to make me a prostitute before the face of God. You should be ashamed! Shame on all of you! If you were a mother to me, you could never demand this from me!"

"Enough bitch!" Marta stamped furiously on the floor, pushing her red face close to Shana's and raising both hands. "Enough! Not another word! If you weren't a bitch, you would never say this to your mother's face; if you weren't prostituting yourself, you would not get on your high horse! Loving and caressing! *That* is what you are after. Any other honest girl would be ashamed to say that to my face, but you, you are proud of it! You will do what I want, what I tell you, or I will throttle you like a puppy. You will not make a brothel of my house! I am your God! You bitch! I am your mother, I gave you birth. Had I given birth to a stone rather than you, it would have been better!"

"What a wooden mother you are! I have no mother. From this day, you are not my mother! You can kill me, but you will not sell me. I spit on what the village will say, because the village is outwardly pious, but inwardly a villain and a harlot. They are white-washed tombs! I would prefer to be killed immediately than become an 'honest' harlot, which is what you want to make of me!"

"Shut up!" Marta shrieked, grabbing Shana by her head and beating her mercilessly. All the rage that had been gathering for days now burst forth with elemental force, demanding to be unleashed. Blows were falling upon Shana's head; she tried to protect herself, but feebly. Red in the face like a lobster, Marta yelled and hit Shana on her head, until she fell down on the floor.

Had Joza not arrived home, who knows what she would have done to Shana in her terrible rage. But his arrival prevented further beating. He grabbed hold of her hands and pushed her aside:

"You are going to kill her! Have you gone mad?"

He helped Shana to get up and sit on the bench.

"I'll kill her before she brings shame on me, before she makes me go mad!"

"Let there be peace for once in this house! I long for peace! What sort of life is this! You are not to lay hands on her again. She would go mad with your beatings!"

"I will beat the devil out of her! If she wanted to go mad, she'd have gone mad by now!"

"Everything can be worked out in a nicer way, because violence begets violence. You can achieve nothing by force."

He sat beside Shana and took her hand in his, but she moved away and, with disgust, removed her hand from his. He noticed it and felt stung to the heart. He felt a deep abyss had opened up between Shana and him, and he felt that she despised him. Suddenly it dawned on him how horrible and obscene was their violence, and for the first time he felt pain and anxiety in his heart, whilst looking at Shana dishevelled, weeping and beaten-up. He wanted to say something kind and comforting to her, but he did not know what to say or how to console her.

Shana got up and went outside to the front of the house. Marta looked at her from head to toe, and spat after her, whilst Joza bowed his head in thought.

A gloomy autumnal light seeped in through the window. The church bell rang out and its sound filled the village with the reminder that it was midday and time for lunch. Outside everything looked festive and peaceful. Sunday noon entered the village with smiles for the merry householders, but the door of Joza's house was closed to it and this Sunday noon did not bring the peace and joy of God's blessing to his house. Hankering after happiness had kicked out happiness itself. Instead of the sun of love burning brightly, only the green flames of hatred and contempt blazed on.

Chapter 14

That which he had secretly feared, had finally happened. He believed to the end that he would win, that no matter what, she would defy them all, but it was now becoming clear to him that their influence was crushing her, and that slowly and surely she would be left at their displeasure and mercy. Autumn shed the leaves from the branches, yellowing the grassy paths. Marin walked through the fields for a long time, but he did not see the autumnal splendour: he did not see the subtle beauty in the gradual death of the flora – the beauty that softens the heart and leads to nostalgia. The fields were left empty and bleak, covered with stubble far and wide; the waters of the streams, yellowed. Above the woods heavy clouds gathered, and the birds flew past quickly. There was a sharpness in the air, and the wind carried the spiders' strands, now high, now low down to the ground. Marin walked through the woods, and now and then he would sit down on a fallen tree and he would give way to the thoughts that hounded and ensnared him. Wherever he sat down, Shana's image was before his eyes, following him with every step and to every place. She was always there, before him, so real, her presence wherever he was. Sitting on a fallen tree with his hands propping his chin, he stared at the ground before him without seeing, and he asked himself how it could be that there was no law against this injustice done to the two of them. Was there no law that could protect against parental despotism; that could show the face of justice? Why so many written laws if not to make people happy? And God? Why did He permit things like this, why did He keep quiet in the face of the groaning and weeping of the poor? Why did the powerful threaten others in the name of

God and the poor console themselves in Him? Why was the honest heart always filled with bitterness, whilst power and injustice adorned themselves with the symbols of honesty and magnanimity? It was a lie, a colossal and dirty lie, that all people are equal. There was no equality. These were empty and invented words, of use to some. The bigger the thief, the better he prospers. If you are rich, justice is yours, you can hold your head high and your deeds are honourable. But the poor man seeking justice has to pay, justice has to be paid for, and the more you pay, the more just you are.

Such were the thoughts that preoccupied the mind of Marin, and the open wound of his soul bled profusely and nothing could heal it. At dusk, when the fields slowly sank into semi-darkness and the daily life of the village quietened down, he returned home and, without a word, sat down in his room. There was no peace anywhere for him. He longed for it, but it was far, far away. There were moments when he grabbed hold of his head and chest in despair, when black and terrible thoughts plagued him. In his thoughts he saw his victims lying in a pool of blood in pain and him standing above them without remorse, because he did not feel he had committed a crime. He stood, and as he left his room and saw through the window a weak reddish light he remembered his mother and all the trouble she would have to face if he took his revenge. The thought of his mother dispersed the black and bloody thoughts. She was the only person worth living for and sacrificing his life for. She was the only light point in his life, the only value that was not lost to him. He knew that she could not live without him and that his revenge would kill her, and so because of her, he did not take revenge. Her weak and almost blind eyes needed a leader and her poor life needed a guardian and protector. And he was her leader and her protector.

He no longer went to the village. He avoided company. He lived alone, far from village life. He had become disgusted with its gossip, its insinuations and intrigues. He noticed that his mother also suffered because of him and therefore he tried to hide his pain, burying it within him, so that his mother could again become cheerful and content. He undertook any job, thinking he might forget through work. Thus, whilst in the evenings other young people continued to meet and stroll in the streets, singing love songs, giving vent to their boiling passions, he would lean on the doorpost and stare into the night that approached from afar. He ventured nowhere nor did anybody come to see him. At this time, the village carried on as normal. The time of weddings began, new intrigues, new sins and new crimes that were never going to be punished by any human law. Quietly and wantonly moaned the violins at weddings; food and drink were consumed to exhaustion; people shed tears and cursed fate and the hour they were born; they rejoiced and cackled, as money and land were glorified.

At this time Mika's house, too, was getting ready for the wedding feast. The cellars were full of good wine, the granaries full of wheat, and the lofts full of maize. Mika was in a good mood, with renewed strength in his veins, because the harvest of the land was a strong and powerful support on which to build his future with certainty and without fear. He had become particularly tyrannical and insolent ever since the Sunday of the first reading of the banns in the church, when he was told how pale and lost Marin had been upon leaving the church that morning. Mika's power in the village returned unscathed and his reputation grew. No one judged him any more, no one was bothered by his past behaviour, all that remained was a great human envy and desire for the same kind of power, the same kind of wantonness and prestige. Only the occasional soul looked at Mika with contempt, and even fewer would outwardly express their disgust with a slight shrug of their shoulders. Days were passing, life went on in its usual way. On Sundays there was dancing and drinking in the pub, and wives cheated on their husbands and swore before God and the world that they were pure and unsullied defenders of family happiness and family morals.

All this time Marin was experiencing a different spiritual suffering. Loneliness was driving him to the one thought in which he could find no relief for his soul. And suddenly a desire to get drunk took hold of him, so he could forget everything. Thus, one day he went to the pub, sat at a table and ordered half a litre of wine. As the night progressed, the pub became more crowded. Cigarette smoke rose over the uncut hair, fur caps, and greasy hats. It was Saturday evening. People were talking loudly at other tables, whilst Marin sat quietly engrossed in his own thoughts, drinking glass after glass.

Nobody took any notice of him. The flame of a large paraffin lamp hanging from the ceiling cast a reddish light on the walls and faces, and the cacophony of jumbled words increased in volume. Everyone complained about something. Nobody was satisfied. But they quenched their dissatisfaction with good wine and their futures with the nebulous hopes of drunken stupor. Marko, the son of Martin, who had gambled away about thirty acres of land, was trying to convince those present that he saw with his own eyes the Bishop receive, every morning, a packaged newspaper, one copy only, specially printed for him. When he was asked where the newspaper was from, he winked slyly, importantly struck his forehead with his forefinger, and pronounced imposingly:

"If I knew, I would not be sitting here. You can't find out about these things just like that."

"What packaged newspaper? He lies!" somebody shouted.

"What do you know, you misery?" yelled Marko in reply.

"I have experience. I understand politics. It was not for nothing that I was once arrested by detectives. Not for nothing was I in prison!" responded the other.

"What for?"

"I was suspected of being a Russian count, I was so like him, they said."

There was a sudden uproar. Suddenly, there was uproar. Everybody was guffawing and shouting, calling him a liar, and saying that his snout looked more like a pig trough, and that a count's suit would be as good on him as a waistcoat on a hog.

The room resounded with laughter, Marko was yelling something, and though his mouth was opening wide and he was clenching his fists, his voice could not be understood.

At this moment the village musicians arrived and started tuning their instruments. Matija Sertich, Marin's good friend, followed the musicians in. As soon as he saw Marin, he approached him, shaking hands with him and asking after his health. Marin was surprised, but welcomed him and asked him to sit beside him. Having asked for another glass, Marin poured the wine and raised the glass to Matija.

"I am so pleased to see you," said Matija. "It's been a long time since I last saw you. Where could I have seen you anyway, when I have been busy all this time? Lots of work, one doesn't know where to start first. And how are you?"

Marin shrugged his shoulders:

"As you see, I live."

"You have changed," Marin's friend told him. "You look thinner. I hope you are not ill?"

"I do not know myself what is wrong with me," replied Marin. "I live, but it is a miserable life. It is better if one doesn't think about it. The man who thinks more, suffers more."

"What is wrong? Has some misfortune befallen you? I have not been to the village for several months, I've been on the farmstead all this time, I do not know what has been happening in the village."

"I do not know whether it is misfortune, but I feel everything is upside down inside me. I prefer to tell you myself rather than you hearing from others. Shana had the first banns read with Mika."

"With him?" Matija was startled and grabbed hold of Marin's arm.

"With him."

"That is disgusting! Indeed, that man Joza deserves to be strung up in the middle of the village! To force her to marry, to use force to sell a Christian soul!"

"What can you do? Nowadays this is honest, this is clever. Really clever. But I am stupid and mad, worth nothing, I am not a man. Can you believe it, that I am not a man? Do you believe this lie that people are equal? There is no equality!"

Marin spoke with great bitterness, drinking glass after glass and ordering another litre of wine.

Whilst they were talking, the musicians finished tuning their tamburitzas and started playing quietly. The sound of the violins and tamburitzas was soft and tender. At the other tables, people clinked their glasses together and drank their wine thirstily. The sound of music drove them into a world which never became real to them. It aroused in them that which was so far away; so longed for, but never attained, awakening in them the pain for the beauty that had been so short-lived, so illusory. The singing spoke of things anticipated and desired so much, but which everyday life had stripped bare by their self-denial and disappointment. And whilst the music swarmed mercilessly over old hidden wounds, gazes strayed to somewhere far away, chairs twisting and squeaking, hands falling down onto tables and gripping glasses, fingers in a feverish clench. Then they moved over faces, adjusting hats to the nape of the neck, restlessly combing hair until, finally, long-hidden secret sighs issued from deep within their chests. When the singing stopped, only the clinking of glasses could be heard as the wine slipped down their hoarse throats, intoxicating them. Then they shouted and yelled, demanding more music. And they were given more! The room was thick with smoke, choking the breast and dimming the eyes, whilst glasses were being smashed on the floor.

Marin watched all this from the sidelines through a fog of cigarette and the smell of wine, and he felt that with all of the others he was receding into a dark and vast distance, without pain, where one feels that a disembodiment to nonexistence enables the calming down of one. And now, in drunken haze, with bloodshot eyes, now he felt the pain that troubled him somewhere far, deep inside, as long-gone, barely remembered any more, hurting no longer, even as it made one sad and drowsy. And all this played before his eyes like some diaphanous and greyish fog. He cast a glance at the hands holding his glass. He thought of his life, his work, his mother, and his daily torment. He was alive, yes, but what was this life? What had his life been so far? He started working for another man in his childhood. He worked till the evening, his youth and his sweat drenching another man's land, filling another man's granaries with wheat; and yet he himself had remained poor, a perpetual servant. Though he was a hard and honest worker, never sparing his strength, it was never enough for them. And when the time came for payment, they complained that he asked for too much, that he ate their bread, and that the work he did was barely worth a mention. He would stand silently, looking at the ground. It pained him that on more important occasions they saw in him only a servant, valuable only as long as he was healthy and able to work. They failed to see the man inside him, with his rights and dignity. A worker was only ever a worker, even if he was cleverer and a better soul than his master. The master was always right.

The events of his earliest childhood passed before him. They passed quietly, as if they wanted to remind him of something that would never return, could never return, even as it continued. His whole life had been pain and hard work for someone else. He so longed to be treated as a human being, to be appreciated and to have his rights respected. However, the rights belonged to the rich, they were clever and worthy of respect. He had worked for many years, but achieved what? His house was slowly falling down, the eaves shedding, only brown bread on his table, but the master got richer, extended his house and yard, and bought several acres of land. He had learned that by honest work alone, man could not prosper, and that the bitter bread he had been earning was devouring a part of his youth. And now they robbed him even of Shana, who had been the sole hope and support of his life. His life was bearable only if it had some meaning but when all that meaning had been taken away, all hope shattered and emptiness left in his chest, then his life became only a heavy burden and a terrible torment.

The red wine slipped down his throat. His eyes looked out through a foggy membrane and his hands trembled and stopped as if they wanted to go elsewhere. On another table, laughter broke out, and then a dreadful silence and a sound of moving chairs.

He heard somebody ask:

"Why don't you get married?"

Another voice, half-drunk, answered:

"It is the easiest thing to get married."

"I expect you would get married if a girl wanted you. But you are not wanted by anyone! Who could possibly love such a horrible man like you?"

"Right, the important thing is that *you* got married. I do not have to."

"You will never get married. If you were any good, you would have a wife, but you are incapable, you are not a man."

Laughter accompanied those words. But it was very brief.

A bang filled the room.

A large wine bottle hit the wall and broke into smithereens. A wooden chair flew back, hitting the table, ending up in the yard. Some people jumped to separate them. Others immediately pushed their hats on and disappeared into the darkness.

In a moment, peace had settled again, the only reminders being the breathless and incoherent voices trying to interpret the unexpected event. The musicians put their instruments away and were preparing to leave. Within half an hour, Marin was alone in the pub. He put his head into his hands, lost in thought. The publican pulled up his chair and sat beside him, but he pushed his glass away and got up, leaving without a word.

Outside it was a deep night. The long street lay peacefully under the sky strewn with stars. And below the houses, long shadows rested and gathered together mysteriously, as if they were cold and wanted to stay close for warmth. Somewhere in the distance a dog barked, briefly and sharply. Then two night-watchers, armed with rifles on their shoulders, walked past. He continued to walk slowly on his way. He heard only the even and dull steps that rustled after him, following him like a faithful dog. An inner stillness engulfed him. Nothing pained him. Nothing disturbed him. He felt this calm rise within him, unknown to him before, and with it an indifference towards everything. He would have liked to have sat down somewhere and remained thus forever without moving. He would have liked to have closed his eyes in sleep, never to wake up. His body felt tired out. When he got home he lay down on his bed, placed his arms by his sides, surrendering to something he did not recognise. He wanted to sleep, but sleep would not alight on his eyes, a light smouldering inside him that would not be denied. Loneliness, cold and vast, began to descend upon him. His eyes opened, floating empty in the darkness, the alcohol having filled his veins and the distant ache having started to flood in like a painful feverish warmth, wrapping itself around him with its soft murky arms.

In the morning he awoke with a headache. His head was heavy like stone. He noticed his pale sunken form in the mirror. He needed to go to work at the farmstead, but he felt indifferent to everything. He took a few bites of his breakfast then put his spoon down.

His mother watched him anxiously, and asked him in a trembling voice:

"Marin, I am worried about you. You are sick, aren't you?"

"I'm not, Mother."

She came close to him. She placed her hands on his head and caressed his hair. Her voice was full of concern, caring and warm. And whilst she talked, he felt there could be no person in this world that he might compare her to.

In the afternoon he went to the farmstead. The master of the house received him angrily:

"I have been waiting for you all day and nothing! So much work to do! Now is not the time for courting."

Marin did not answer. He threw his jacket over his shoulder and went to work. The farmhand who looked after the horses, as soon as he saw him, winked at the servant woman nearby and said:

"Are we off to the wedding shortly?"

Marin glared at him:

"It would be better if you minded your own business."

"We thought you were inviting us to the wedding. And you are getting angry. Well, what a bridegroom you'd make!"

Marin threw his jacket on a tree stump, and stood still:

"Leave me alone!"

"Your anger is wasted on us. What can one do? One has to work. A servant is always a servant. When you marry Shana, you will be a rich master, you will not have to work!"

Marin's face became grim. The words twisted like a knife in an open wound. The injustice that he was disregarded by everyone, despised wherever he went, finally got the better of him. Suddenly he found himself holding a fork. The farmhand had barely recovered from his speech, when he felt a dull thud on his head and fell down on the ground. The servant woman screamed, running into the house. The household gathered around in fear. Marin took no notice of them. He threw the fork away and said with contempt:

"Here is your invitation to the wedding!"

The owner's wife started screaming:

"He's killed the man. Oh! Blood is pouring from his head."

"What is happening?" the rest of them shouted.

"Move away!" the owner ordered, moving himself close to the servant who had fainted.

The servant woman was trembling and telling everyone what had happened, for the third time, holding onto her bosom as if she were out of breath. Everyone was surprised. They just could not imagine how Marin could have done something like that. Never in his life had he harmed anyone and here now he had nearly killed a man. The owner was angry at first, and then he became serious as he paused to think. When the servant was carried into the room, and his head wound was cleaned up, and after he came to, the owner asked:

"What happened?"

"You can see for yourself."

"He could have killed you. And what for?"

"Almost for nothing. I just made a joke and he attacked me immediately with the fork. Who could have expected that of him?"

The owner's wife kept berating Marin, demanding of the owner that he dismiss him at once, because she could not abide a criminal under her same roof, capable of killing all her household.

The owner found Marin in the vineyard. He was sitting on a tree stump in front of the wooden cabin, staring into the distance. His face was pale and drawn. When the owner stopped behind him, Marin did not turn around, as if he were not there.

The owner coughed a little to draw attention to himself. Marin continued to stare into the distance.

"Here, light up," said the owner, offering him a cigarette.

Marin took the cigarette, feeling it with his fingers, and lit up.

"It is a beautiful day," the owner continued. "Thank God, we have finished all the important jobs. It is getting colder now. Winter is not far off. There is another job that needs doing, that wood near the fence needs to be cut, chopped and put away. Anyway, you have nothing to do now, you could do it as a bit of fun."

"I could," replied Marin.

"The saw is under the coach-house," continued the owner.

"I know."

"You can finish it by the evening if you work hard."

"Today is not a working day," replied Marin.

"Why not?" asked the owner.

"People take rest on Sundays. There has already been enough hard work during the rest of the week. It is only right that a man has some time off."

"Do you not eat on Sundays? He who eats, needs to work also."

Marin discarded the half-smoked cigarette and turned around:

"I know my duty. Even if I am a servant, I am not cattle."

"Well, yes, it is so. You have had your food in my house, you have been clothed and now you have become aggressive. You even started killing my servants. That is not nice. If you have become bored in my house and do not like it when I refuse to listen to you, you can walk free, wherever your heart takes you. My door is always open. I will not stop you. I was good and just to you."

"Thank you for such goodness and justice! Do not worry, I am leaving. It cannot be worse in other places. You shuddered over every mouthful I took, you feared I would eat you out of house and home. Though when it came to work, you did not know when it was enough. Give me what I have earned. You know what we agreed."

"You ate my food, I clothed you, I even gave you money occasionally. So what else do you want? I think our accounts are settled and there is nothing more to add."

"What?" Marin jumped and stood up before the owner. "Is that our agreement?"

"If you do not think that is right, you can charge me!" said the owner, turning his back and returning to where he came from. Marin watched him, his bottom lip trembling. He felt like running after him and knocking him down and smothering him like a newborn kitten. Just to show him what justice looked like and what its price was. His chest was heaving as if he had run uphill quickly and so he stopped, gasping. He clenched his hand, threatening the owner:

"I shall seek justice! If I cannot find it anywhere, I will create it myself!"

He turned around and cast a glance over the fields. The Sunday afternoon was resting over them. They lay there, long and wide, without crops. They awaited the winter to cover them with a white blanket so they could sleep and rest. They wandered a long way into the distance, but they encountered no joyful twitter of birds, and no blue flowers blossomed beside them. Marin looked at them, thinking how often he had traversed them, either driving the sheep or carting the wheat or hay home; how late in the evening he would return home so tired. These fields took his early youth, soaked his sweat. And now, when he had finished with the harvest and stored it in the owner's granary, now, he could go, as he was no longer of use to him. And what about the payment for his labour? Had he not earned anything? And the agreement? Did that no longer stand?

He turned around and went back to the owner's house to collect his things. At the doorstep, the wife met him. She looked at him with contempt, up and down:

"You savage! Shame on you!"

He held onto the doorpost:

"Why should I be ashamed?"

"And you even ask? You killed an innocent man!"

"Did you hear what he said to me?"

"It does not matter what he said to you, you shouldn't have hit him."

"So I should have kept quiet and allowed him to walk over me?"

"You could have killed such a good young man. Oh, my goodness, what have I lived to see in my own house? And what else is in store for me from my ungrateful servants? Instead of kissing my hand because I am better to them than their own mothers, they yell at me. Pick up your few rags and get out of my house, I cannot bear to look at you!"

Marin dropped his hand from the doorpost. An imperceptible smile touched and twisted his lips:

"Do not be so vexed, I did not kill him, he won't die."

Then he tied up his things and, throwing them over his shoulder, he went towards the vineyard, whence he went down to the village. Before he descended into the valley, he paused and looked back. He looked at the farmstead and the trees around it. His heart was heavy. He had spent so much time here, and now he was leaving. Well, more driven away like a stray dog from the doorstep. Why were they driving him away? What had he done wrong? He had defended his rights! He had pointed out that he too was a man. That frightened them, they were flabbergasted, because they thought that a servant had no rights: it was his to work and obey. How suddenly it had all happened! How terrified these loan-sharks were of man and truth. But he would seek his rights, for justice must be somewhere.

He bent down and adjusted the bundle over his shoulder. He descended slowly to the valley, treading the loose soil in his soft-soled leather shoes. The autumn sun shone above him, but in his heart was bitterness and pain.

He walked with his head bowed, deep in thought, as if he was looking for a place where he could deposit his heavy burden, a burden that had been loaded onto his back by the inhumanity and injustice of man. Only his tracks remained behind him, tracks which at dusk the dark shadows would descend upon, dragging him into the depth of the night and oblivion.

Chapter 15

Autumn days were beautiful.

The skies were clear during the day; the nights resting in the full moon and the stars twinkling charmingly. The rains had stopped, the water trickling through the narrow channels in front of the houses down to the valley. The paths had hardened and the cart tracks were well-rutted in the hard soil.

At this time it was all busy in Mika's house. The village women would work from early morning. Some cleaning rooms, some polishing furniture, others making cakes and doing the roasts. Everyone in the house was in a state of urgency. Mika was here and there overseeing the work, pretending to be busy and as if interested in everything. The women teased him with their double-talk, drinking and laughing loudly, because he failed to see the slivovitz on the sly.

With a flask in his hand and decked out in all his finery, the wedding crier was inviting neighbours and relatives to the wedding. He went through the village raising his glass to passers-by, winking at them and moving on. Out of sheer curiosity, many women came nosing around the house, asking all sorts of questions, so that they would be able to gossip in the village about what they had heard and seen in Mika's house. It was already circling in the village that the next day there was going to be a wedding celebration and that Mika was going to marry Shana! The whole village was buzzing with the news and everyone was in a state of tense expectation to see the wedding party of all wedding parties. Many were looking forward to the plentiful good food and drink, with the women impatiently offering their opinions about Mika and Shana; however, the maidens, with apprehension in their hearts, pondered on Shana and her unhappy love, fearing that one day the same fate might befall them.

Mika laughed a lot, pretending to be cheerful, but as soon as he was left on his own, he would scowl. He kept looking at the ground and it was obvious that something was troubling him, worrying him secretly. He did not confide in his mother, as he knew he would find no understanding there. She was dead against this marriage. He knew it would be useless to talk to her about his feelings after the bitter wrangle, when he had yelled rudely in rage at his mother and left her appalled in the room, slamming the door after him without thought. He remembered how she had warned him in a harsh and rather ludicrously tearful voice not to marry Shana under any circumstances, for she was going to find him a better girl. She was going to find a girl from somewhere as long as he obeyed her and did her bidding. But he would not hear of it. Neither her pleading nor her protestations nor her tears made any difference to him. He was adamant and he told her that he was going to do what he intended, even if it all came to grief. He also reminded her that everybody always spoke ill of a bride-to-be, putting it down firmly to the wagging of evil tongues. And he did not care a hoot what other people thought. But when she started to plead with him again and, in the end, threatened to throw herself into a river, or, in her old age, take a cane in her hands and leave for the wide world, he became so angry that he swore at her and yelled at her, without any consideration, that he was the master in the house, and it had to be as he wanted, even if the devil's eyes fell out. For those who were not happy, the doors were open, and they could leave, he would not stop them. Though she threatened to leave, she did not leave but stayed and withdrew into herself as if plotting something. At times he would look at her surreptitiously and when in the end he noticed that she joined in the activities with the hired women, even so something eased in his soul, as he thought that after all she had become reconciled to his decision, because she was certain that she had no other way out.

When she went into the garden and sat on a bench, he made to join her, but he changed his mind and returned. At that moment, the door opened to reveal Joza with a whip in his hand. Shaking hands with Mika, he asked:

"Busy I see?"

"Busy. All working. It will be all ready for tomorrow."

"That is good. But have you reached an agreement with the musicians?"

"I have."

"And the wedding guests? How many will there be?"

"Who could know? As many as will come."

"Good, good," replied Joza. "The important thing is that the work is being done. I just called to see how you were doing. I arrived in my cart. I am off to the farmstead to collect some things, but I will be back tomorrow in time for the wedding guests to collect the bride. I am off now."

"You cannot go yet!" Mika stopped him. "Where is that bottle so we may drink to our health!"

They clinked glasses and took a sip of slivovitz. Mika, seeing Joza off, returned to the room but immediately went out again. It was obvious that he was restless. In thought, he sat on the chair outside the house. In his thoughts, he saw Shana. He saw her sitting at the window and doing something. His glance lingered on her beautiful hands, over her shoulders, her face and hair; his heart softened and in his soul he felt something pleasing, awakening in him a secret desire to draw her to himself and to embrace her. But she raised her eyes and her angry glance, full of contempt and hatred, pierced him mercilessly. He felt it like a stab to his chest.

As he was occupied with these thoughts, he suddenly got up from his chair and, joining his fists behind his back and walking thus, he started thinking about how he would tame her the moment she married him and entered his house. Everything then would be different. He would know how to treat her. He would break down her obstinacy and she would obey him, for she would see that he is a man and it has to be thus and it cannot be otherwise. He would conquer her hatred, and this hatred would turn into obedience and submission. Why should she hate him, he would tell her, when he loved her and would hand over all his worldly goods? He would fulfil all her wishes, whatever she desired, no matter what. One way or the other he would win her over, for there is no woman who cannot be won over by a man, as long as he finds a suitable way to make her indebted to him through some magnanimous act of his own. She would forget Marin, as have so many others forgotten their sweethearts when they married another. Life makes us forget.

Whilst thinking thus he also remembered Marin and feared subconsciously that he might come and take revenge. And at the most inopportune moment. He might appear suddenly from nowhere and kill Shana or him, and then everything would be finished. No matter how often this thought troubled him, he kept rejecting it as nonsense and tried to convince himself that Marin would not dare do that, believing that he would have to accept his fate and bow his head in submission. Well, after all, he was not so stupid as to commit a murder for a woman. He would destroy himself forever and destroy his mother, too.

Mika began to calm down with thoughts like these and he felt a joyful warmth spreading through his chest. He suddenly sensed that he had only just discovered the joy and beauty that had previously been hidden from him for so long. Everything around him had become more beautiful. The yard was bathed in the sun, trees were standing proudly and the horses were in high spirits, neighing in the stables, as if they too awaited the next day with impatience. The warm hay smelt sweet and it reminded him of haymaking and the times when he himself had walked through the tall grasses, breathing in the fresh and delightful scents. His spirits rose so much that he felt like a child intoxicated with restless expectation, opening both arms and running towards the one from whom he expected to receive a gift.

The following day, the wedding guests already began to arrive early in the morning. They came in their richly embroidered clothes to show off their status and their standing before the world, wanting to be seen and heard. Young and old, women and maidens, young men and children – all were pouring into Mika's yard, cramming themselves into the rooms, demanding drinks and laughing raucously, and whooping madly and wantonly, in order to give vent to their hidden instincts that were to be celebrated today. Their faces expressed joy, their eyes a subdued flame, waiting for the right moment to turn into a blazing flame. In front of the house, young men drank and sang, pushing back their hats decorated with flowers and multi-coloured ribbons. The main door to the house was wide open, the curious already gathering and watching from the sidelines with a lively interest in the events unfolding inside the yard. The wedding guests continued to arrive in decorated carts, harnessed to the frisky horses that raised their heads, pawing at the ground and waiting for their bridles to be loosened so they could take off along the village streets, welcoming this quiet and great morning, full of a sunshine with the promise of a glorious day. There was not a cloud in the sky. The day was unfolding the best as could ever be hoped for.

Whilst the wedding guests were arriving thus, greeting one another, asking after their health and news, in a cart the musicians also arrived, and the circle-dance immediately started up in the yard. In the meantime, Mika was getting ready in his room. He put on his brand new black suit, tailor-made for the event, and a pair of brilliantly shiny new knee-length boots. In his lapel he wore a rosemary nosegay, evocatively scented. He moved back and forth in his room as if looking for something, though he was not aware of what he wanted. Casting a quick glance in the mirror, he adjusted his hair and his suit.

When his mother entered the room, he grasped both of her hands, and looking deeply into her eyes he said joyfully:

"Mama, be joyous! Rejoice because you have lived to see your son get married. I will bring you a daughter-in-law into the house: a help, vigour, and youth."

"If one waits long enough …" she said, with tears in her eyes.

From the yard the whooping of the girls could be heard and the music wantonly carried the circle-dance on its wave, and already even the women and men began to join in. Mika glanced through the window and, seeing them, he trembled with emotion and pride because they were rejoicing on his account. They came here to give vent to their hearts, for this was Mika marrying today, the first amongst the young men, with many a girl's heart secretly trembling on his account. But what about him? He played them and cheated them without feeling pain, without longing for any of them. And now he was going to show them again that it would be as he wanted, as he had previously decided, when people were saying in the village that Shana would never be his, that she would never love him, and that he could never persuade her to marry him. He would come before them with pride and full of self-confidence: let them look at him, let them be envious of him and let them speak who he was and what he could do!

Cart after cart was arriving at the yard and he heard a song, sung by one of the girls:

"Sweetheart of mine, handsome and tall

my heart quakes when before me you sprawl.

Sweetheart of mine, and my lamb too

our secret fondling left us in a stew."

The music sobbed quietly now, as a torrent that subsides and then erupts with a greater power to break down all obstacles. Another girl's voice was heard:

"My sweetheart, my dove

has dark eyes sparkling with love.

I love him, does he love me,

the gossips will not leave us be.

Sweetheart of mine – or not,

get wed, finally tying the knot!"

Then a woman rendered a song:

"What a blessing, a wonderful sight

to see your son take a good wife."

But the young men did not want to be outdone by the girls. So throwing their heads high, full of pride, clicking their heels and glancing around, one of them started *his* song:

"Ducats out of fashion,

acres and tipsy rogues are in.

Mama, give us another son,

you shall have two rogues instead of one.

Little brunette, you are so young

or I'd marry you with no dowry anon."

Mika listened to this song, watching them all and smiling, and would have loved to join them in the circle-dance and the singing. He knew them all, both male and female. They were born here, had grown up here with him, had had fun and had drunk and partied with him. They had shared their hopes and fears with him, longing for something new, great and good. And now they were here, they had come to celebrate his last day of bachelorhood. How he now found them so dear and close!

The sun was rising. The day arrived in the village with brilliance and clarity, as if it were Sunday. All was festive and irrepressible, all was ebullient today.

At 10 o'clock the wedding party was ready and, along with Mika, they took to the streets accompanied by music and song to fetch the maiden.

Whilst all this was going on in Mika's house, Shana sat speechless in her room. Her eyes were red with deep shadows, and pallor and exhaustion marked her face, but hardly any tears. She sat as if condemned – without thoughts, without feelings. She was numb and she hardly registered the severity of the cursing and invectives that her mother poured upon her head, calling her all manner of rude names. The whole night long, Shana had not been able to close her eyes. The whole night long she had begged not to be forced to marry Mika, but to no avail. Her mother did not understand the weeping of her daughter. But it was not only her mother, but her relatives too, all of them telling her there was no point to what she was doing, that she was ruining herself. Happiness was smiling at her and she was kicking it away. They could not even imagine in their dreams how she could be so stubborn. She, a grown-up and clever maiden, how could she thus behave like this! In spite of all this, Shana refused to listen to their entreaties. Beforehand, she already knew every thought and word of theirs. She had heard them so often that their very repetitiveness became like a heavy weight upon her chest, threatening to choke her. She wanted them to leave her in peace, so she could breathe and rest. But they were persistent. Shana felt as if a huge, dark abyss was opening up before her, into which they were pushing her, and that all her resistance was in vain. Whilst her mother was bridling up to her, bending and twisting her arms, she did not even want to look at her. But when she did glance at her, seeing her scowling, distorted face, she asked herself: was really her mother, this woman who knew only how to scold and curse, this woman who was talking to her of some maternal sacrifice, love, sleepless nights? Was this her mother?

The warm rays of sunshine entered through the window-panes into the room and fell on Shana's face, spilling down over her bosom and the hands that rested in her lap. On top of the big table they lit up the new dress that she would have to wear to the wedding, the freshly picked flowers that would adorn her hair, and the trembling tiny shiny mirrors that would shimmer in her decorated plait. But she had no desire to look at the table, for she could not imagine that the day had indeed arrived when she would have to part with all her treasured hopes, with everything that seemed beautiful to her, everything that was waiting for her somewhere. No, this wedding dress was not hers, she did not imagine it thus. It was all alien to her, including those women coming and going with their looks full of reproach. She wanted them to leave, she did not want them to stand here looking at her. She wanted them to leave her alone so she could be alone with her thoughts. But these faces did not leave. They continued to look at her with curiosity and expectation. She felt like jumping up and hitting them in the middle of their foreheads, to scratch them and send them packing. She was startled in the middle of these thoughts by her mother's harsh, acidic voice:

"What are you waiting for? Get up and sit in front of the mirror. It is time to get dressed. You cannot wait here until midday. People have arrived. I hope you do not expect me to kneel before you and beg you to obey me? Come on, get up! The women in the hall are waiting for your call to get you dressed for the wedding. We cannot wait any longer. Well, at least today you should not be so obstinate to bring shame on me. What has to be, has to be. We cannot avoid our fate, we cannot run away, it will catch up with us, no matter where we run, no matter how much we protest. What can one do, it is fate!"

Again, Shana saw only a vast and deep abyss. With the utmost effort she knelt down in front of her mother, and raised her clasped hands:

"I beg you, before God, leave me alone, do not force me to marry Mika, I shall go mad! I beg you, as I never begged you before in my life, free me from this agony and disaster! If you ever loved me, if you considered me your child, listen to me, do not destroy me! Do this as I ask and I shall be grateful to you to my dying day and I shall bless your every step and I will kiss the soil you walk on. Do not throw me into this abyss, if you are my mother and you fear God, for you must know He will judge you justly one day!"

Her pale arms were raised high in supplication, her voice trembled expressing all the misery and despair of an abandoned and misunderstood soul. This was her last attempt at salvation, the last twitch of the victim offered up to parental tyranny. It was the final call to the humanity and integrity of her mother's love, this cry was a comment of a pure heart that was breaking and despairing, because it finally grasped that there was no understanding from those she thought were her nearest, those who would protect her and be prepared to sacrifice everything for her happiness.

Her mother started pulling her hair out and yelling in despair:

"I wish God would have struck me blind, I wish the thunder killed me, rather than to see this shame brought on me! And by whom! My own blood! I curse every word I babbled to you, I curse every mouthful of food I fed you with to bring you up! You are bringing shame on the house, a shame unheard of in the village or in the world!"

"Mother!" Shana burst out sobbing and clasped her mother's knees. "Do not curse me! Do not curse me and do not send me into the world without your blessing! I shall obey you. Do with me what you will, I will not resist any more. Let it be as you wish, maybe it is preordained! Only, do not curse me!"

Her tears no longer flowed down her cheeks. Her face became pale, flooded with a crystal-clear white, as if it had become flint. Deep, icy peace entered her whole body, like a frozen silence. The last hope that had kept her going was now snuffed out. There was no more hope. A vast and dark emptiness flooded her soul and a loneliness not known to her beforehand overwhelmed her. All that was beautiful, humane, her belief in love and trust in human beings, was shattered. She realised that profit was stronger than anything else. So this was the real life as lived. Everything else, but everything else, was only a lie. And this mother's love and integrity and humanity, all this was a lie, that had been used to cover up the real truth about life, that hid the rottenness and bestiality of the human spirit!

She sat in front of the mirror. The women came and dressed her. They adorned her plait, laying it around her head with flowers and shimmering tiny mirrors, and on her bosom they placed large red "grains" and a big red rose in the middle of it.

The women knew exactly what to do, as if this were the only work they ever did. Singing could be heard from outside. These were Shana's female friends singing in the yard and in the other rooms of the house. She grasped the words of the song, she knew the tune very well, but at this moment it all seemed very strange to her. No, they did not sing for her now, it was not her song. She did not expect a song like that. Her song would never be sung again, it would never pass any lips again. It would remain buried, far away, surmised and never realised.

"Hurry up!" Marta said. "I can hear the wedding guests coming. Almost here. They will get here any minute now."

The women are bending over Shana. They are adjusting the flowers in her hair to make her more beautiful and more desirable to the groom. They straighten her embroidered top, multi-coloured belt and the bustle behind her back, falling from the belt. She is sitting, not moving. She surrenders to them: let them do what they will. She no longer feels either joy or sorrow. A great emptiness yawns in her.

"Look, they are entering the yard!" commented the womenfolk, looking through the window.

"They have arrived."

"How many are there?" others commented.

"How handsome and proud! How happy the mother who has lived to see her child happily settled! What joy, indeed, for the parents!"

Shana stood up. She looked at them in a composed and cold way, and said:

"What are you waiting for?"

"Good luck!" the women responded.

"I am ready. If you have waited for me, let them enter. I am ready."

The women looked at each other without a word.

"What a beauty …!" whispered some amongst themselves.

Marta motioned the women to leave the room. She took Shana by the hand and walked her to the door. The door opened. Mika stood at it in his wedding suit. Their eyes met. Mika's eyes revealed longing and joy whilst in Shana's eyes lay a weighty calm. Mika looked at her enthusiastically.

"Shana!" he exclaimed.

"You have come to take me?" Shana responded calmly.

"Yes, to take you. To take you, to be mine alone. To take care of you and to make me happy!"

"You think you will be happy with me?"

"I hope so."

"No, happiness is not possible here. Had you been a man, you would have left me in peace, you would not have destroyed me. I am marrying you because I have to. I have to because I do not want to be cursed. I have been sold. But my heart, my heart will never be yours."

Mika bowed his head, thinking to himself: "You will change. I will teach you how to treat your husband!"

"I am here! Take me!" Shana said, looking at him coldly.

He turned round to look for Marta in the other room, but she appeared directly behind him.

"Where is Joza?" Mika asked.

"I expect he is somewhere around. I have not seen him since yesterday when he went to the farmstead, I have had that much to do. I will go and find him. I am sure he is in one of the rooms with the wedding guests. I will fetch him to give you his father's blessing."

She was about to leave when a frightened woman with an expression of horror in her face stood in front of them:

"It is evil! A great evil!" she said breathlessly.

Everybody looked astonished.

"What evil? What are you talking about?" Mika responded with agitation.

"They are bringing him in the cart. They have killed him ..."

"Whom? Speak!" Marta was trembling.

"Him. Joza."

"Oh!" Marta began sobbing and ran into the yard.

The doors were wide open. Suddenly a dreadful calm descended. In the whirlpool of enjoyment, horror settled. The cart slowly entered the yard.

The police brought Joza to the wedding of his daughter. He was lying on his back. Blood was pouring from his head onto the damp hay. His eyes were half-open. The coagulated blood was on his lips. His breathing was laboured and intermittent. He was brought into the room and laid on the bed. The doctor was quickly summoned. When he arrived, he discovered the wound to be very serious, and warned of the worst. The blow had been delivered to Joza's head, which had rendered him immediately unconscious.

Utter horror rained on the house. At first, nobody even thought of the possible killer, at least Mika and Marta did not consider it. They were mostly concerned that the wedding might have to be postponed if Joza died. Therefore the wedding must go through before Joza breathed his last. The invited guests were bewildered and became quiet. Fun ceased and the music went silent.

Marta directed the wedding guests to the church, without song or music, to get on with the ceremony, so that afterwards, God willing, Joza might recover, maybe the wound was not fatal, and it would be so damaging to postpone the wedding when so much money had been spent on it. Mika also agreed with this suggestion, and thus immediately the wedding party went slowly and silently to the church, as if they were going to a funeral.

In the whitewashed village church, which had stood for decades on the elevated ground, and which gathered people under its wing on Sundays and Holy Days of Obligation, in this church Shana married Mika before the ordained priest. When the wedding party turned to go home, having barely left the church, the news of the death of Shana's father arrived …

Chapter 16

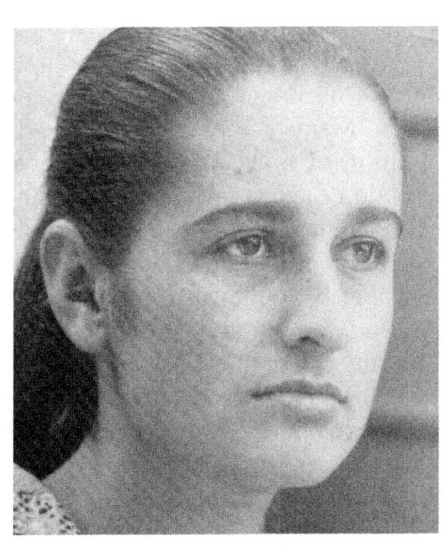

The news of Joza's death spread quickly, not only in the village but also around the nearby boroughs. The authorities immediately took matters into their own hands. Everybody asked: who is the murderer? Suspicion fell on Marin. Everybody said that Joza could not have been murdered by another but Marin. Everybody deemed that he must have done it out of revenge and nothing else. It was well-known that Marin loved Shana, that finally he was rejected, and in order to give vent to his hatred, he must have murdered Joza. Precisely on Shana's wedding day.

The authorities immediately arrested Marin. It was expected that he would confess his guilt at once, but he objected, insisting that he had nothing at all to do with this murder. He had not sunk so low as to dirty his hands with the blood of the monster and heathen who had sold his own daughter. However, as a defence this was very weak. The authorities refused to accept it. No guilty man ever confessed his guilt readily, endeavouring with all his might to get out of the trap. Not only did Marta go round the village shouting with raised arms that Marin had killed her good and unforgettable husband; not only did Mika speak spitefully, insisting that he could swear Marin was the murderer; but suddenly the whole village jumped up and declared that Marin was the guilty man and therefore had to be punished. Such a man might not and could not live in the village, because anything could be expected of him! Whenever his name was mentioned, women would spit scornfully on the ground and men would shake their heads in suspicion. Nothing like this had ever happened in the village before.

There in the town whither Marin was taken, the trial was in process; sentence was to be passed. Many witnesses were called from the village to give their opinion of him. All of them were eager to comply with the invitation, and really enjoyed the prospect of expressing before the Court what they thought and what was in their hearts. Only Shana trembled and nearly fainted when she learnt that she too was called as a witness. The day was fixed and the invited arrived. When Marin was asked where he was when Joza was attacked, he answered that he had been at home. But he could not confirm this statement with any proof, as nobody had seen him at home. True, his mother confirmed it, but which mother would not speak up for her son? He had no proof that he really was at home at that time, and not in the field lying in wait.

Some witnesses spoke about an incident a few days earlier that he had wanted to kill a worker in the place of his work, and that this was the reason he had been sacked by the owner. The owner himself confirmed it. Moreover, others said that they saw him that evening going to the field with a stick in his hand, gloomy and angry, never raising his head. One of the witnesses even swore that he saw Marin run across the field on the same night that Joza was killed. Two more witnesses came forward claiming that they saw him near the village in the early hours, even before sunrise, looking very pale and frightened and passing them quickly as if afraid of them. The Court listened to all the witnesses. All of them told of their suspicions and the possibility that Marin had killed Joza, because only to him was Joza bloody before his eyes, and because of him Shana had married Mika. Some of them told the Court of Marin's threat to kill Joza to exact revenge. And of course Marin remembered that at one point he had said that in front of others in rage. The Court accepted this as a premeditated action to carry out his crime. Nobody was found to be a witness for Marin. He was all alone. He swore in vain that he did not kill

Joza, that he was innocent. The Court could not take his word for it without proof. Proof was needed, not empty words.

At last Shana's turn came. Utter silence reigned in the Court. Everyone waited tensely for what she was going to say. Mika's face reflected a gloating smile. He was sure that Marin was hurtling towards a disaster from which he could never extricate himself.

In answer to the Judge's question, Shana raised her head and said firmly:

"Marin is not a murderer."

"All right, have you any evidence?" the Judge asked.

"I have no evidence, but I feel that he is innocent."

This statement of Shana was not sufficient. Evidence was needed and there was no evidence to confirm Marin's innocence. All spoke against him. And now when Shana said that he was not a murderer, they were all dumbfounded, not knowing what to think of her. How could she feel that he was innocent, how dare she speak out like that in front of everybody, now that she was Mika's wife?

Finally the Court gave a verdict. Marin was to be sentenced to fifteen years in the dungeons. When the sentence was read out, he heard it standing. He felt as if he were sinking into a vast dark abyss, from which he would never exit. It seemed somehow ridiculous to him. How could they have sentenced him, when he knew he was not guilty? Or maybe this was some sort of a bad dream, from which he was about to wake up and breathe a sigh of relief? But this was no dream. Immediately the gendarmes took him away, and the people went back to their homes, interpreting the sentence in their own ways.

Shana arrived home with difficulty. She dropped on the bench in the room, as if her legs had been cut away. Before her eyes, the Court scene when Marin's sentence was read out was constantly replaying. She saw clearly the misery in his face, so deep and great; she noticed the scorn of all those who spoke against him. He appeared to her as a martyr who was laden with a cross on his back to carry. She could not despise him, though a thought crossed her mind that maybe he could have killed her father. She was only too well aware that he was sentenced to prison because of her, and if she had not existed he could have been happy today. Had she been stronger, had she refused Mika, this indeed would not have happened. However, in the end she had caved in, caved in before her cursing, and he, in despair, had raised his hand to the one who had destroyed their happiness. No, he was not guilty, he did not kill her father; she did, because she had lost her courage, she was not strong enough to resist them and remain at all costs steadfast, to be herself. Only now, from her stupor, which was engulfing her, did her eyes begin to open, did she realise what had really happened. But it was late. Dark and endless pain gnawed at her inner self. She saw their lives as a total failure. His youth would be spent in the prison and she would suffer and be tormented here.

Mika could never forgive her because she was the only one, and now as his wife, who had spoken up for Marin. He maltreated her mercilessly day after day, wanting to take revenge on her for his misery, for he felt now that she was not his, though she had married him. Even her mother treated her with scorn and goaded Mika to control her better, for she might bring further shame on him. And he needed no goading. But neither words nor beatings changed Shana. He saw that she was not his, though she had married him. It pained him to see that in the depth of her soul, she despised him and was disgusted with him. He had so hoped that the wedding would have achieved all that.

When he would return home drunk and irritable, he would come to her with bitter accusations of bringing shame on him, before the world, by thinking even now only of that murderer. And when she kept silent and wasn't opposing him, he considered it a challenge and he would raise his hand to her, ready to finish her off, in order to assuage the rage and misery that filled him more and more.

Days were passing, but there was neither peace nor happiness in Mika's house. Shana withered and suffered, and her mother rarely came to see her. When she did come, she brought neither consolation nor support but fanned the flames of even greater dissent.

She would speak to her alone:

"What is wrong with you, you misery?"

"Nothing!" Shana would answer coldly.

"What do you mean, nothing? If it were nothing, you wouldn't be as you are? Can't you see where this is leading? Why don't you use your brains? You are not a silly child any more, you are a woman, act like one. Is it possible that you are still infatuated with that murderer? Do you still fail to see what he has done, or will you remain blind all your life and drive me to an early grave?"

"Why don't you leave me in peace? Why are you torturing me? And anyway, what do you still want from me? Did I not marry Mika? Did I not do as you wanted?"

"You did do it, but you must change towards him. You are his wife!"

"Yes, I am his wife, but I cannot stand him. You can kill me, but I cannot love him, I cannot be different towards him."

"You do not have to love him. Do you think I loved your father? But you can fawn on him, you are a woman, with fawning much can be achieved. Look to make it better for yourself, enjoy your life, do not trouble your head about anything else. Twist him around your little finger and you will see what a meek lamb he will be. Women can do anything. You only have to know and want. Once you have twisted him, it will be easy for you with him. But you are stupid and stubborn and you refuse to be sensible. I am telling you this because I want the best for you, because I am your mother. Nothing can be achieved by what you are doing!"

When her mother left, Shana thought about her words. Her throat tightened at the thought of behaving as her mother had been telling her to. How could she behave like that when she felt something totally different, when her inner self rebelled wholly against it?

Mika's drinking got worse. He took to coming home very late at night, cursing and yelling and running after Shana to beat her, chasing her out into the yard where she would spend the night. He spent money recklessly. He played cards and lost a lot of money on the cards. Those who kept his company praised him and flattered him that he was the first man in the village, that he could do what he wanted and that there had never been nor ever would be an equal to him. It tickled his vanity greatly and he continued to pay for drinks, because when Mika partied, the drinks flowed. The invited and the uninvited would drink and money was spent, and acre after acre was sold.

In this way, two years passed and Mika was left with a few acres, but he refused to stop the extravagance. Others more prudent saw that he was recklessly running towards disaster, but nobody could prevail upon him to stop. Some pointed the finger at him, others at Shana. At the end of the third year, Mika demanded of Shana that she sell her land to give him money, because he needed the money. However, she didn't want to sell the land. If he spent his, he would not hers. He was persistent and would not give up. He needed money, money, money, but there was none. So he demanded a loan from Shana's mother. In the beginning she would lend to him, but later when he refused to repay she refused to hear anything about lending, nor did she go to his house any more. He yelled at her, accusing her of forcing her daughter on him, as a result of her thinking that she would have had it made at his, that she would have enjoyed whatever he had. But she was very wrong, because Mika was no fool, Mika knew what he had taken on and what life was all about. Just you wait, she would give him the money: if she did not, he would chase her daughter back to her home, letting the whole village see what she was like. However, not even this threat was of any use. Marta would not hear anything about money. She had no money to throw away. Let him grow wiser, live sensibly and honestly, and then he would not need the money.

Shana's life was very hard in these circumstances. She never heard a nice word, no understanding. Only hatred, threats, curses. She longed for light and peace. But there was no peace. Often she pondered about everything that had happened, her thoughts often turning to the days when she was happy, at least for a while, and that fed her soul. She firmly believed that justice was to be found somewhere and that one day it would come her way, freeing her from this suffering. At times she thought it could all have been different, that she could have been so happy and content, if only her parents had wanted to understand her. But the important things for them were the land, the riches! And now look at how much land her father has now. That small piece that they buried him in was enough. Shana's eyes filled with tears thinking about how her father had ended up. Well, he had no understanding of her heart, but he had been her father after all.

Shana did all the work, in order to somehow forget everything, and to find some contentment in her work. His mother scowled at her, because she was convinced that this evil was Shana's fault. In this way she wanted to justify Mika, but she did not succeed. He turned on her too, being rude and harsh, as if she weren't his mother. He spoke in a manner that was horrible to hear.

One night, as the darkness settled on the village, when the sky was cloudy with a fine rain falling, Mika was again drinking in the pub. The musicians were playing as if possessed, the tables again full of wine, and there was drinking and merrymaking. Glasses and bottles flew to the corners of the pub, broken glass all around, jumbled up voices shrieking wantonly and loudly. It was well-known: Mika was partying once more. But it was not known from where he had got the money. His company was not interested in that. The important thing was that the money was there, along with the drink; the rest was of no import to them. Female singers appeared from somewhere and joined them. Mika, in an expansive mood, ordered everybody to accompany him to his house to continue with their merriment.

Shana heard the music from a distance. She got up from her bed, went to the window and stared out into the darkness. She hoped Mika would be drunk again, but she had not envisaged what was actually about to happen. The gates flew open, the drunken party burst into the yard yelling and screaming. Mika led them. Barely on the doorstep, he started yelling:

"Open up, you bitch, when your husband arrives!"

Shana came out and faced him.

"Bring the wine on, we want to celebrate, we want to drink! What are you staring at me for, as if you had seen me for the first time!"

The party burst into the room. The musicians were singing and playing horribly. The female singers were wrapping themselves around Mika. He sat them on his knees, ordering Shana to serve them with wine. But Shana stood by the door, staring at him silently. That enraged him. He picked up a chair and swung it in order to strike, but one of the female singers grabbed hold of his arm, and the chair missed. Shana ran quickly into the night. Mika continued to swear and yell, but having taken it in that Shana was gone and was not serving the wine, he ordered the horses to be harnessed to the cart and driven through the village from pub to pub. They all agreed to this. The horses were ready in no time, and the party piled onto the cart along with the musicians. Mika brandished the thin leather whip and the horses took off as if on wings. The clatter of the wheels of the cart in the night sounded ghastly, and the screeching voices of the drunk songsters sounded horrendous. The villagers got up from their beds to look at what was going on in their street at that time of night.

They watched in astonishment, women crossing themselves and saying that this year the hail would destroy all their crops and that some evil was going to afflict the village. But for those who were having fun, the most important thing was to enjoy themselves in order to please Mika. Mika was particularly high that night. He drove the horses pitilessly, their mouths foaming, and the cart jumping up and down on the uneven and dangerous path, creating a terrible racket.

The darkness was getting thicker, the wind blew swiftly along the street, and big drops of rain began to fall. Mika wanted to turn into a side street at the greatest speed, but the front wheel stuck on the stone that was supporting the bridge, under which water flowed. In a flash, the cart overturned, the singers and musicians strewn on all sides. The horses panicked and carried on for a few metres, and then, breathing heavily, they stopped. Those thrown out picked themselves up and, yelling, went to look for Mika to continue. They found him underneath the cart. His head was bleeding. They struck matches to see better and to lift him out, but it was late. His torso lay under the cart, and across his neck lay the ladder. Blood was pouring from his mouth. They quickly freed him from underneath the cart. As soon as they saw what had happened, the female singers quickly disappeared, frightened, filthy and wet. The others placed him on the cart and took him to his house, unconscious. All the doors were wide open, but there was nobody anywhere in the house. The chairs were strewn about the room. They kept calling for Shana and for Mika's mother, but they were nowhere around.

Only silence and a cold odour of something unpleasant and odious lingered in the rooms. Outside the wind blew hard, and the rain was falling as if the skies had opened ...

Chapter 17

The suddenness of Mika's calamity shocked the whole village. Nobody expected anything like this, least of all Shana. When she heard that Mika had found his death under the wheels of a cart, and when she saw him lying there, she burst into tears, sobbing for a long time. He was dead. He had killed himself, because he had had no respect for his limits.

After his burial, Shana moved in with her mother, who sued Mika's estate, because he had not returned the money borrowed from her. She became different towards Shana. She could see for herself how in the last three years Shana had visibly declined and become but a shadow of the former Shana. Her mental anguish had been far more crushing than the physical.

Even so, Shana began to regain her peace as she lived her new life. She breathed a sigh of relief, because she no longer feared being beaten or abused by anyone. On Sundays she would go to church, praying earnestly and devoutly to God to have mercy on Marin, to help him, as it was not his fault but hers. She prayed for him to be spared as he had ruined his youth because of her. She took upon herself all the jobs in the house, with her mother. Withdrawing into herself, she did not go to the village. The truth was that since Mika's terrible death, everybody looked at her in a different way, because they considered it to be God's finger, God punishing him, she herself feeling no inner need whatsoever to come into contact with the village. She had comprehended what and how the village was, and had developed a repugnance towards these small-minded people, who enjoyed and gloated over the misfortune of others. But had it not been for this village with its views and ways of life, and with its mercenary morals, today she would not have found herself in this situation.

Barely six months had passed since Shana moved in with her mother, and again suitors came calling. True, they were not exactly exciting suitors, and she refused them all, because it was clear to her what their reasons were. Her land remained whole and untouched, and Mika had only a few acres left. She was certain that the suitors did not come for her but for her land. Even had they come for her, she could not have responded, as there was nothing in her inner self that could tie her to them.

Days were passing quietly, as they did in the village. As time went by, a shadow of oblivion began to cover past events. The village carried on living its old way of life. It lived as always, and hoped for something better and more beautiful.

Winter was coming to an end and spring was approaching. Here and there small patches of snow were present, but they soon melted, water trickling through the narrow little channels below the village, brushwood bursting into leaf, branches starting to bud, the grass turning green, and the sun reawakening everything into a new life.

In the fields, the heavy ploughs churned the black earth in some places, the horses' nostrils fuming with a warm white steam like burning incense, whilst the earth deep in its bowels anticipated the shuddering of a new power, of new life.

Sometimes Shana would herself go to the fields, inspecting the land and working alongside other workers. And in the evening on her way back home, she would think of Marin and wonder how he was. She felt in her soul that it was certainly very hard for him, that he was suffering. She had flashbacks of all that had happened in these fields, remembering the meetings with Marin, and of all the beautiful hopes that had raised her heart heavenwards. And then, then, before her eyes, would come the Courtroom, her dead father, and the bloodied Mika, and anguish and a deep pain would settle on her bosom, and she would sigh, bow her head, and carry on. Even now, after everything, it often seemed to her that life was impossible, and in these moments of temptation, she had to fight herself not to give in, and to find a way of accepting even a life like this. She knew she had to live, but she often failed to see the meaning of her life. These were the hardest moments of her present life. But then there were times when it seemed to her that even this life of suffering was so beautiful, because through it she entered more deeply into herself. These were the profound silences after which even greater storms and a greater tearing asunder would occur.

In this way, her life was passing between those silences and the inner battles. She had already accepted that she would not see Marin again, when something happened that shook the whole village once more. Like lightning, the news spread in the village that Joza's real murderer had been found at last and that Marin was innocent. It struck the whole village like a thunderbolt. Immediately, the question arose: who is the murderer, who is the murderer? Then those who had borne witness against Marin swore loudly that they too were convinced that Marin had been innocent and that they had always been prepared to take an oath to prove it. Immediately, people wanted to know who had brought the news and then whether the news was really true. Soon, everything was revealed.

Here is what happened:

A few days previously, Martin Pavich entered the pub, and started drinking and complaining that he could no longer live like this. He could not go on, because he could not bear the voice of his conscience, which had been pursuing him at every step. He looked unwell, he had neglected his wife and children, and if he earned a little bit of money he would spend it on drink immediately, in order to silence his inner voice, but to no avail. He had waited for Joza and killed him, and not Marin. He had killed him and fortuitously got away. He had killed him to take revenge on him for that poor roof that Joza had sold over his head and for throwing him out of his own house like a dog onto the street. True, he had not intended to really kill him, he had just wanted to give him a beating, but he had hit him so awkwardly that it proved fatal. And he had not wanted to kill him, it would have been a sin to have a worthless dog like that upon his soul, but regretfully that's how it happened.

The authorities quickly heard about this. The case was looked into and it was confirmed to be true. The eyes of the village were opened. Who could believe it? Marin, being innocent, had served over three years and more in prison. Now he was going to be released and return. Barely a week passed, and even the newspapers brought the news that Marin had been released, innocent, to his freedom. Women felt sorry for him, for his having sat in prison unjustly all that time, and men pondered and shook their heads saying that everything in the end comes out. If not today or tomorrow, in the end it has to come out.

When Shana heard that Marin was coming home as innocent, her hands trembled, tears of joy flowing from her eyes, and she felt that in her was growing a great, endlessly powerful, and beautiful life, opening up before her. "He is innocent! He is innocent," she spoke excitedly, pacing the room and then the yard, not finding peace anywhere. She could hardly believe that he would return, that she would see him again. But suddenly a thought and an uncomfortable feeling touched her inner self. How would he receive her, how would he look at her?

Perhaps he would despise her, as she had betrayed him? And what was there for her, a poor soul, to look forward to? What could she expect and how could she dare to hope for anything from him? She married Mika, having broken her word, and now how could she hope that he still loved her, that she was still dear to him? How could she even entertain thoughts like these? Then, again, she would be comforting herself with the thought that he was returning, that it would be better and easier for him. But immediately, she would think that there was nothing beautiful waiting for him any more in the village. His mother had died in the first of his imprisonment, because the poor soul had not been able to bear such a blow. His house was half a ruin, the thatch falling off it, everything neglected. He would be returning to his hearth like a man whose house had burnt down, poor as a beggar.

There would be no one at the doorstep to meet and greet him, and be joyful at his return.

The sun was shining, the days unusually beautiful. Nature again breathed its warmth and vigour of life, people devoting themselves again to work. Evenings were full of warm scents, cheering the soul, nights were balmy and delightful. It was one of these evenings when Marin, carrying a bundle on his stick, arrived below the village in his yard, after he had been freed. Tears filled his eyes, because he found his house empty, his hearth without flame. He remembered his mother and they way he was told how she died, and he felt an even bigger weight. It was necessary to start again, it was necessary to roll up his sleeves and march towards a new life.

When the village heard that he had arrived, they flocked to see him, to admire him and praise him, but he could barely listen to these words. They could awaken nothing pleasant in his heart. What's more, he was disgusted with them, for he knew their fickleness and triviality. The boss, for whom he had worked before, came personally to say he was happy to offer him his job back, the job which the owner was very sorry he had left of his own free will, but Marin simply laughed, rejecting that kindness. He lived alone, withdrawn, in his poverty. He bought a cart and a horse and started tilling his small plot of land again.

The wheat had already grown quite tall in the fields. Summer was in full swing. The sun burned mercilessly, the birds flew around, and patches of water turned into big shimmering mirrors. The ears of wheat were full, they promised a good harvest. Everyone was looking forward to God's blessings. Marin walked through his field with rolled-up sleeves looking at his land. And he pondered about this land that fed the good and the bad, and he saw that it was better and more beautiful than people. It alone remained true and devoted, all the others had abandoned him. Had the land betrayed him, what could he have done? The golden ears of wheat awakened in him a quiet joy, his nostrils flaring as he breathed in the blessed scent of the land and the fruitful crops. He felt that something profound and strong bound him to this piece of land from which he drew his strength for living.

In the evenings when he sat alone at the table to eat his bread, he remembered Shana and everything that had connected him to her. He remembered vividly the scene in the Court, when she had been the only one to say that he was innocent and not a murderer. Her witness had touched his heart deeply, it had been a strong support and a great consolation during the days of his suffering and trials. He felt that his feelings for her were not dead, and that she continued to live in him, but he did not know whether she had become indifferent and disappointed with life. He knew that she was as rich now as she had been before, and that he was poor, he knew that she had loved him. He wanted to see Shana to ask her how she was, because he had heard that she had suffered a great deal. For a long time he wondered what to do. He saw that even now the land stands between them, that it separates them, along with one life of suffering which has brought new insights to them.

One evening when he could no longer bear it, for a disquiet was preoccupying the whole of him, he put on his best suit and went straight to Shana's house. When she saw him her legs trembled, and she grasped the wall with her hands, turning pale. Marta was also surprised and stood there without a word.

"I have come, Shana," he said, "to see you, because I could no longer bear this. If you still feel anything for me, if I am not dead to you, marry me without anything. I do not need anything. I have two strong hands, I am still young, and I will work and feed us. Life has not deprived us of everything, we can still live and we can still be happy!"

His words were trembling as if torn from the depths of his soul, his eyes shining. There was a ghastly silence in the room and now, as in the past, the clock on the wall ticked indifferently.

Shana was trembling. She wanted to say something to him, but the words stuck in her throat and she began sobbing as never before.

Marin came closer to her:

"We have suffered a lot, everything has passed, the sun will shine at our door too. I did understand you, I could not despise you, as I knew how you felt."

Marta was shaking from some inner agitation:

"Marin," she said, "can you forgive me, for I myself see now how much I have wronged you, how much in error I was. And now, I myself see that there is something more valuable, more beautiful, and stronger in us than riches, than this damned selfishness and greed. And I was convinced that you killed Joza. I can see how much in error I was, and I can also see what sort of happiness Shana had in marrying Mika. Two hard-working hands and a noble heart are worth more than an ocean of riches! I wish to God that my eyes had been opened to that before, if only they had everything would have been different!"

"What can you do, perhaps it had to be thus! None of us knows what awaits us. We are all human. The important thing is that we are alive and healthy, and with God's help our life will become beautiful again ..."

Shana was sobbing. Marta's eyes filled with tears too.

Marin took Shana by the shoulders and enfolded her in his arms:

"Do not cry, after the rain comes the sun," he said, as his own tears flowed down his cheeks ...

The End

Biography of the Author

Ante Jakšić (Bereg, 22nd April 1912 – Zagreb, 30th November 1987) was a Croatian writer, poet, story-teller and novelist from Bačka, East Croatia.

He was a teacher of Croatian language and literature. He was one of the greatest Christian poets in Croatia.

Although he was an excellent sonnet writer and lyricist, and the author of the most popular novels amongst the Bunjevac and Šokac Croats, with the arrival of the Tito's Communists in 1945 his creative writing was simply banned and the literary critics of the time ignored him, because his work was imbued, amongst other things, with Christian views and themes.

He was a member of the Christian Literary Society of Sts. Ćiril and Method, the Society of the Croatian Writers, a member of the Editorial Board of the Literary Review of Marulić, and he edited a book titled "At the Sunday Dinner Table" – on the works of around thirty poets.

In his native village he finished six grades of the Elementary school and took up the locksmith trade, but soon left and went to the seminary opened by Bishop Lajčo Budanović in Bač.

As a seminarian, he took private classes at the Subotica High School (a grammar school). He attended the fifth and sixth grades at the Archbishop's classical High School, which was run by the Jesuits in Travnik. He completed the seventh and eighth grades of High School in Sombor (1932). Then he went to Zagreb, where he took up Slavic studies & Roman studies at the Faculty of Philosophy. He finally graduated there.

After becoming a teacher of Croatian language and literature, he worked as an educator in Travnik, on the island of Badija near Korčula; then in Tuzla, Osijek, Beli Manastir, Slavonski Brod, Gospić, Subotica, Karlovac and Zagreb.

In 1982, he received a charter from St Pope John Paul II, in recognition of his long-term Catholic activity and on the occasion of Jakšić's 70th anniversary of his life and the 50th anniversary of his work.

He died in Zagreb in 1987 and was buried in his native Bereg.

Printed in Great Britain
by Amazon